THE SEED OF EARTH

In a dark cave, on a cold planet, in a distant galaxy, four Earthmen sat and pondered the chance that had sent them there. The Computer had picked them to carry human civilization out beyond the limits of the Solar System. They were to be pioneers of a virgin world.

Four humans, imprisoned in a cave by alien raiders, awaiting an unknown fate, watching for the inevitable crackup that would hurl each at the others' throats —knowing that whatever they did would determine the future of their colony . . .

THE SEED OF EARTH

ROBERT SILVERBERG

Hamlyn Paperbacks

THE SEED OF EARTH
ISBN 0 600 38314 8

First published in Great Britain 1978
by Hamlyn Paperbacks
Copyright © 1962 by Ace Books, Inc.

Hamlyn Paperbacks are published by
The Hamlyn Publishing Group Ltd,
Astronaut House,
Feltham,
Middlesex, England

Made and printed in Great Britain by
Hazell Watson & Viney Ltd,
Aylesbury, Bucks

TO ROBERT BLOCH

INTRODUCTION

The science fiction world of the late 1950's was an odd place, a kind of fallen empire that had collapsed into eerie provincial decay. There had been a big publishing boom in s-f from about 1949 to 1953, with dozens of new magazines founded, the first rush of paperback science fiction, and even some activity on the part of large hardcover houses like Doubleday and Simon & Schuster. Then most of it fell apart. The magazines died in droves, because there simply weren't enough readers to go around. (In 1953 alone there were 39 s-f magazines, which was about 35 too many.) The paperback houses, having madly overextended themselves in their first hectic period of expansion, sent hundreds of millions of unsold books to the pulping machines and cut back drastically. And the hardcover people who had dabbled in science fiction found that sales were trifling; Doubleday stayed in the business, but nearly all the others dropped out.

Against this background of retreat and retrenchment I began my career as a professional writer, circa 1955. I would much rather have been starting out during the Golden Age of 1949–53, when new writers were desperately needed to fill all those blank pages, and spectacular careers were launched overnight by such beginners as Philip K. Dick, Robert Sheckley, and Algis Budrys. But I was too late for the gravy train, and I had to make do in the very much reduced circumstances of the next era.

Strange things went on during those pinched, dark years, and the publishing history of the book you now are holding provides a revealing look at how young writers coped with the situation that existed then.

THE SEED OF EARTH began as a short story, some 9000 words long, called 'The Winds of Siros.' I wrote it in March of 1957 for a magazine called *Venture*, published by the same house that published *Fantasy & Science Fiction* and edited by Robert P. Mills. *Venture*, which had come into existence late in 1956, was an interesting project that deserved a better fate than it met. Its aim was to publish strong, hard stories, intense and robust; unlike all the rest of the science fiction magazines of the time, it was unafraid of the erotic forces, indeed wanted its writers to acknowledge that human beings did other things beside pilot spaceships and invent time machines. And yet it was not just a magazine of sexy slam-bang pulp adventure fiction. It demanded literacy of its contributors, grace of style, intelligence of story construction. Since it was free of the taboos against sex and forthright characterization that afflicted its competitors, many writers who felt constricted by the timidity of the other magazines gladly offered outstanding work to *Venture* for a very modest fee. During its lifetime of only ten issues it ran such splendid fare as Theodore Sturgeon's 'Affair with a Green Monkey' and 'The Comedian's Children,' C. M. Kornbluth's 'Two Dooms,' Walter Miller's 'Vengeance for Nikolai,' Algis Budrys' 'The Edge of the Sea.'

Venture was very much to my taste, for even as a fledgling writer I was concerned with such things as narrative intensity and emotional depth. In 'The Winds of Siros' I did a story that combined a standard s-f theme – the struggles of a bunch of human colonists against hostile and bewildering alien beings – with something that was a bit new to the field, a study of human psycho-sexual interactions under circumstances of stress. The original story began at a point in what is now Chapter Eleven of the novel THE SEED OF EARTH, and took place entirely in the cave where the four captive humans are penned. I liked the story and so did editor Bob Mills, who used it in *Venture*'s fifth issue.

And then I set out to make a novel out of it.

By the summer of 1958, when I began seriously think-ing of expanding my short story to book length, I had already written eight or nine novels, though I was still in my early twenties. Nearly all of those books had been Ace Double Novels – a publishing curiosity in which two novels were bound in one cover, upside down relative to one another, so that whichever way you turned the book you were at the front of somebody's story. Donald A. Wollheim, the progenitor of the Ace Double Novel, had seen some promise in me and had encouraged me to the extent of a book contract every three or four months all through 1957 and 1958. But I was growing restless with Ace. I was tired of having my books published with someone else's book tacked to them. And Ace, valuable market though it was for a hungry young writer, offered little prestige compared to Doubleday, or to Ballantine, the only other paperback house doing science fiction at the time. Doubleday and Ballantine published books by Asimov, Heinlein, Sturgeon, Bradbury, Clarke. Ace gen-erally published books by – well, kids like Silverberg, Phil Dick, Alan Nourse. Ace also published books by Asimov, van Vogt, Simak, de Camp, and others of that rank, but nevertheless there was something vaguely minor-league about the whole operation then. I wanted to get into the big leagues.

I remember taking a long walk before dinner through upper Manhattan one amazingly humid evening in July or August, 1958, wrestling with the unfocused ambitions and yearnings that were troubling me; and by the time I returned home from the restless stroll I knew what I would do. I would turn 'The Winds of Siros' into a novel and sell it to Doubleday. Although when dealing with Don Wollheim at Ace it had been sufficient to turn in three chapters and an outline in order to get the next contract, I would take the risk of writing the entire novel before I showed it to any publisher. I felt that the big-time publishers would scorn to deal with the likes of me on the basis of a portion and outline.

(About this time, I wrote a short story entirely un-related to 'The Winds of Siros' called 'Journey's End,' and sold it to another of the short-lived magazines of the day, *Super-Science Fiction*. When it came out in the April 1958 issue, the editor had changed its title to 'The Seed of Earth.' I liked the new title so much that I ap-propriated it for my expansion of 'The Winds of Siros.')

I wrote THE SEED OF EARTH in October, 1958. It differed from my previous novels in its greater concen-tration on the exploration of character. You may not notice all the searching, probing details of character revelation that I thought I was putting into the book, because there really aren't a lot of those things in it, but I *thought* there were, and certainly my characters were a lot more real than any I had created before. I took the book downtown to my agent, told him it was going to be my breakthrough novel, and instructed him to sell it to Doubleday.

Doubleday turned it down.

That hurt. But they were publishing only one book a

month of science fiction at Doubleday, and I decided they were just too busy doing Heinlein and Asimov to have room on the list for me. Well, there was always Ballantine. This time, instead of relying on my agent, I took the manuscript to Ballantine myself. I had a long and amiable chat with Betty Ballantine, told her all about my ambitions and yearnings, and gave her the book.

She turned it down, too.

I still thought it was a pretty good book – but obviously the big-league publishing companies were simply so pre-occupied with the outputs of their big-league writers that I wasn't going to break into that charmed circle. Okay, I resigned myself to seeing THE SEED OF EARTH appear as one more Ace Double Novel.

But just then one of the outstanding s-f magazines, *Galaxy*, inaugurated a companion line of paperback novels that was designed to follow the old *Venture* policy: strong s-f adventure with a generous component of sex. THE SEED OF EARTH fit their needs exactly, and so my agent let them have the book. The advance was the same as Ace would have paid – $1000 – but the big difference, to me, was that *Galaxy*'s edition wouldn't be a double novel. I'd have a whole paperback all to myself. I had never had that privilege.

I collected a down payment of $500 in February, 1960, and waited for the other half, which was due on publication. And waited and waited, and never got it, because the *Galaxy* paperback series sputtered to a halt and terminated without ever publishing my book. Eventually *Galaxy*, with my permission, recouped its $500 investment by running THE SEED OF EARTH in the issue for June, 1962.

There are a lot of oddities about that. For one thing,

stories in *Galaxy* are supposed to be previously unpublished, but a good chunk of THE SEED OF EARTH had been used in *Venture* only five years before. For another, there had already been one 'Seed of Earth' by Robert Silverberg in a science-fiction magazine, the unrelated story in *Super-Science*; this one confused all the indexers. And, too, when *Galaxy* had bought the novel for its paperback series I had been asked to add a few graphic sex scenes to the original manuscript. This I did; but when the magazine ran the story, it had to be cut for reasons of space from 50,000 words to 35,000. The 15,000 words that went out did not include the inserts I had been asked to supply, which meant that *Galaxy* had first asked me to expand and then drastically to cut the same story, and had ended up publishing an abridged but unexpurgated version!

Amid such confusions did my novel finally see print – some of it, anyway. With *Galaxy*'s ownership of the book discharged through the magazine release, I was again free to seek a book publisher, and shortly my agent found one: Ace. Don Wollheim, who probably would have bought the book willingly enough in 1958, gathered it in finally, after all these adventures, late in 1961, and in the summer of 1962 it reached the newsstands. Yes, as part of an Ace Double Book, but there was one consolation for me: the flip side of the volume was also a Silverberg title, a story collection called NEXT STOP THE STARS. At least I didn't have to complain that some other guy's book was riding with mine.

And here, fifteen years later, is THE SEED OF EARTH again, at last published in solitary splendor. I realize now that it's not the profound mixture of adventure and human insight that I thought it was in 1958, but I still think it's an okay book. And it's interesting to see how many of my later literary themes and obsessions turn up in it – notably the aliens who place human beings in a condition of stress for hidden purposes of their own, which shows up again in *Thorns, Man in the Maze*, and a good many other works of mine. I enjoyed reading it again and I'm not overly embarrassed at loosing this very early novel of mine on the newsstands. I hope you'll find pleasure in it not merely as an historical artifact.

Robert Silverberg
Oaklands, California
April, 1976

CHAPTER ONE

The day was warm, bright, sky blue, thermometer in the high sixties – a completely perfect October day in New York – needing no modification by the Weather Control Bureau. At the weather station in Scarsdale, glum-faced weather-adjustment men were piling into their planes and taking off for Wisconsin, where a cold front was barrelling in from Canada, and where their expert services *would* be needed. Twenty thousand miles above Fond du Lac, the orbiting weather control satellite beamed messages down. In Australia, technicians were completing the countdown on a starship about to blast off for a distant world with a cargo of one hundred reluctant colonists. In Chicago, where the morning mail had just arrived, a wealthy playboy stared at a blue slip of paper with wide-eyed horror. In London, where the mail had arrived several hours before, a shopgirl's face was pale with fear. She, too, had received her notice from the Colonization Bureau.

Around the world, it was an ordinary day, the ninth of October, 2116 A.D. Nothing unusual was happening; nothing but the usual round of birth, death and, occasionally, Selection.

And in New York, on that perfect October day, District Chairman David Mulholland of the Colonization Bureau reached his office at 0900 sharp, ready if not precisely eager to perform his routine functions.

Before he left his office at 1400 hours, he knew, he

would have authorized the uprooting of one hundred lives. He tried not to think of it that way. He focused his mind on the slogan emblazoned on blue-and-yellow bunting wherever you looked, the slogan of the Colonization Bureau: *Do Your Share for Mankind's Destiny.*

But the trouble was, as Mulholland could never forget, that mankind's destiny was of only trifling interest to the vast mass of men.

He entered his office, drawing warm smiles from the clerks and typists and secretaries as he passed their cubicles. In the office, everyone treated Chairman Mulholland with exaggeratel affection. Most of the bureau employees were sufficiently naive to believe that Chairman Mulholland, if he felt so inclined, could arrange their exemption from the world-wide lottery.

They were wrong, of course. No one who met the qualifications was exempt. If you were between the ages of nineteen and forty, had health rating of plus five or better, could pass a Feldman fertility test, and were not disqualified by one of the various social regulations, you went when you were called, in the name of Mankind's Destiny. There was no way to wriggle off the hook once you were caught – unless, of course, you could prove that you were disqualified by some technicality that the computer had overlooked. The remaining child in a family which had lost four or more children to selection was exempt. Mothers of children under two years of age were exempt. Even mothers of children under ten years of age were exempt, if their husbands had been selected and if they had not remarried. A man whose wife was pregnant was entitled to a single ten-month delay in departure. There were half a dozen more such technicalities. But, whatever the situation, sixty ships, six thousand people, left Earth every day in the week. Someone had to be aboard those ships. Somewhat more than two million

Earthmen headed starward each year.

Two million out of seven billion. The chance that the dark finger would fall upon *your* shoulder was inconceivably remote. Even with the figure winnowed down to the mere three and a half billion eligibles, the percentage taken each year was slight – one out of every eighteen hundred persons.

Do Your Share for Mankind's Destiny, said the blue-and-yellow sign that hung behind Chairman Mulholland's desk. He looked at it unseeingly and sat down. Papers had already begun to accumulate. Another day was under way.

His so-efficient secretary had already adjusted his calendar, dusted his desk, tidied his papers. Mulholland was not fooled. Miss Thorne was trying to make herself indispensable to the chairman, as a hedge against the always-to-be-dreaded day when the computer's beam lingered over her number. In moments of cruelty he thought idly of telling her that no mortal, not even a district chairman, had enough pull with fate to assure an exemption. It was entirely in the hands of Clotho, Lachesis and Atropos.

Clotho put your number in the computer. Lachesis riffled the cards. Atropos selected, and selected inflexibly. The Fates could not be swayed.

Mulholland lifted the top sheet from the stack on his desk. It was the daily requisition form. Five of the sixty starships that left Earth each day were manned by Americans, and one of the five American ships each day was stocked with selectees drawn by Mulholland's office. He read the requisition form with care.

REF. 11ab762-31 File Seven.
10 October 2116, notices to be sent.
Assignment: starship GEGENSCHEIN, blasting 17

October 2116, from Bangor Starfield.
Required: fifty couples selected by Board One.

The form differed only in detail from hundreds of
forms that Mulholland had found on his desk at the
beginnings of hundreds of days past. He tried not to let
himself think of days past. He had been chairman for
three years, now. It was of the essence that the high-
ranking members of a selection board should not themselves be subject to selection, and Mulholland had received his present job a few weeks after his reaching the
age of forty had removed his name from the rolls of
eligibility.

He was a political appointee. According to the polls-
ters, his party was due to succumb to a Conservative up-
rising in the elections next month. Mulholland faced his
party's debacle with remarkably little apprehension.
Come January, he thought, President Dawson would be
back in St. Louis practicing law, and a few thousand
loyal Liberal party hacks throughout the country would
lose their jobs, being replaced by a few thousand loyal
Conservative party hacks.

Which meant, Mulholland thought, that come
January someone from the other side of the fence could
sit in this chair handing out selection warrants, while
David Mulholland could slip back into the obscurity of
academic life and give his conscience a well-needed rest.
It was a mere seventy days to the end of President Dawson's term. Mulholland shut his eyes tiredly. Barring a
political upset at the polls, he would only have to pass
sentence on seven thousand more human beings.

He buzzed for his secretary. She came at a gallop; a
bony, horse-faced woman of thirty who ran the office
with formidable energy and who never tired of quoting
the bureau slogan to visitors. She probably believed the

gospel of Mankind's Destiny implicitly, Mulholland thought. Which didn't give her much comfort when she pondered the ten years that lay between her and freedom from selection.

'Good morning, Mr. Mulholland.'

'Morning, Jessie. Type out an authorization.'

'Certainly, Mr. Mulholland.'

Her agile fingers clattered over the machine. In a moment or two she placed the document on his desk. It was strict formality for him to request and for her to type the paper; mechanically, Mulholland scanned it. This had to go to the computer, and any typing error would result in loud and unpleasant repercussions.

As chairman of the District One Board of Selection of the Colonization Bureau, I hereby authorize the selection of one hundred ten names from the roll of those eligible, on this ninth day of October, 2116, in order to fulfil a departure quota of one hundred for the starship GEGENSCHEIN, blasting 17 October 2116. David Mulholland, Chairman District Board One.

Mulholland nodded; it was in order. He signed it in the space indicated, then provided crosscheck by pressing his thumb down against the photosensitive spot in the lower right-hand corner. The authorization was complete.

He handed the form to Jessie Thorne, who deftly rolled it and stuffed it into a pneumatic tube. Mulholland took the tube from her, affixed his personal seal, and popped it in the open pneumotube vent under his desk. The little morning ritual was over.

The tube, Mulholland knew, would drop twenty storeys into the bowels of the building. There, Brevoort, the vicechairman, would ritualistically open the seal, check to make sure that everything was as it should be and then would place the authorization form face-down on a pick-up grid in his office. A photocircuit would relay the contents of the form instantaneously to the computer, that sprawling network of tubes and complexity hidden in the ground at some highly classified location in the central United States.

Activated by the arrival of the authorization, the cryotronic units of Clotho, Lachesis and Atropos would go to work, selecting, by a completely random sweep, the names of fifty-five men and fifty-five women from the better than two hundred million eligible Americans. All five District Boards – New York, Chicago, St. Louis, Denver, San Francisco – selected from the same common pool.

The one hundred ten dossiers would be relayed immediately across the country to Mulholland's office. During the day, Mulholland would go through the dossiers one by one, checking personality indexes and compatability moduli to see if his victims for the day would be able to work together at the job of colonizing a world. Mulholland had learned through experience that he would have to discard about ten per cent of his pick, not exempting them but merely tossing them back in the hopper for another chance. The computer's records were kept scrupulously up to date – a whole beehive of clerical workers handled the job of filing the countless change-of-status applications that came in – but Mulholland could be certain that of each hundred and ten names scooped up by the computer, two would have become ineligible for reasons of health, one of the women would be probably pregnant, one of the men would be psychologically unsuitable. At least once a week it happened that a selected person died between the time of his selection and the time of his notification. Three years of district chairman had taught Mulholland a great deal about vital statistics.

At 0930 hours his names for the day began to arrive over a closed-circuit transstat reproducer. The cards came popping out, five-by-eight green cards with a name and a number at the top and forty or so lines of condensed information typed neatly below.

He gathered them up, stacking them neatly on his desk. Behind him, the slogan warned silently, DO YOUR SHARE FOR MANKIND'S DESTINY. To his left, a gleaming window opened out onto the blue cloud-flecked sky. It was a lovely day. District Chairman Mulholland looked through his names for October 9, notification to be sent by October 10, departure scheduled for October 17.

The selectees had only a week's notice. Fifteen years back, when the star-colonization had begun, they had been given twelve weeks to tidy up their Earthly affairs. But that policy, instituted with the praiseworthy intention of making selection a little more humane, had backfired. Instead of making use of their twelve weeks to tend to loose ends, transfer possessions, pay farewells, some of the selectees had behaved less constructively. A startling number suicided. Others wrought damage on their persons to make themselves ineligible, lopping off hands or feet or putting out an eye or performing even more drastic self-mutilations in their desperate fear of the unknown stars. Still others tried to escape by hiding in remote parts of the world. The three-month period of grace simply did not work. After several years, it was shortened to a week, and selectees were watched carefully during that week.

So Mulholland leafed through his hundred and ten cards, knowing that in eight days most of those people would be heading out on a one-way journey. Mankind's destiny would brook no sentiment.

He buzzed Miss Thorne again. 'I've got the cards, Jessie. Do we have any volunteers today?'

'One.' She gave him the card. *Noonan, Cyril F. Age thirty, unmarried.* Mulholland read through the rest of the data, nodded, tossed Noonan's card in a basket on the right side of his desk, and made a sharp downstroke on a blank tally sheet in front of him. Now there were only forty-nine men to pick for the voyage of the *Gegenschein*. Volunteers were uncommon, but they did turn up from time to time.

Mulholland ran through the men first. He picked out his forty-nine without any trouble, and stacked the six leftover cards in his reserve basket. Those six names would be held aside until it was determined whether or not the other forty-nine were still eligible. If Mulholland could fill his quota without recourse to the reserve basket, the six men would automatically become first on the next day's selection list. Mulholland had no one left over from the day before, as it happened; there had been some trouble filling the October 9 quota, and he had used up his reserve completely yesterday.

With the men's half at least tentatively finished, he skimmed through the fifty female names. Here, occasionally, the computer tripped up. Mulholland winnowed one name out immediately; Mrs. Mary Jensen, 31, mother of four children ages two to nine. She had as much business being in the list of eligibles as the President's grandmother. Mulholland initialed her card and buzzed for Miss Thorne again.

'Have her name pulled from the list,' he ordered crisply. 'She's got a child born in 2114.'

Fate had been kind to Mrs. Jensen. Since her husband had never been selected, her only claim to exemption was that she had a child under two. If her number had come up a month or two later, she would no longer have been entitled to that exemption. But now, because she had been called today, she would most likely never be called again. Probability was against it. Mrs. Jensen was safe, even if she had no more children.

Mulholland prepared the rest of the list. Fifty men, fifty women, with a reserve list of six men and four women. In the afternoon, the notices would go out. They would be received tomorrow morning, and by nightfall, he knew, the useless appeals would come flooding in. None of the appeals ever reached Mulholland's office. They were screened off by underlings, who were trained in the art of giving gentle 'nos'. Mulholland himself had held such a job until getting his promotion to the top.

He looked down the list he had compiled. A college student from Cincinnati, an office worker in San Francisco, a lawyer from Los Angeles. One girl gave her occupation as 'entertainer,' from New York.

It was a cross section. Mulholland privately felt that this was a flaw in the selection system, because very often a group was sent out without a medical man, without any kind of religious counsellor, without any expert engineer or scientist. But there was no helping it. For one thing, it would be grossly unfair to see to it that the computer picked one doctor for each hundred colonists. Generally it worked out that way, but not always.

It was a sink-or-swim proposition. Millions upon millions of stars waited in the infinite heavens. The stellar colonization was a far-sighted enterprise, and, like most farsighted enterprises, was cruel in the short run. But, centuries hence, a far-flung galaxy would shine with the worlds of man. It was the only way. Even though the ships existed to take man to the stars, only a handful of people would consider uprooting themselves to go out into the dark. If the colonization of the stars had been left on a volunteer basis, barely a dozen worlds would be settled now, instead of the thousands that already bore man's imprint. They were small colonies, to be sure, but they grew. Only a handful out of the thousands had failed to take root.

And, thought Mulholland, a week from tomorrow the starship *Gegenschein* would take ninety-nine conscripts and a lone volunteer to the stars. He looked through his cards: *Herrick, Carol; Dawes, Michael; Haas, Philip; Matthews, David;* And eight dozen others. Tonight they laughed, played, sang, loved. Tomorrow they would no longer belong to Earth. The inflexible sword of colonization would cut them loose.

Mulholland shrugged. He was making his old mistake, thinking of the conscripts as people instead of as names on green cards. That way lay crackup. He had to remember that he was only doing a job, that, if he didn't take care of it someone else would. And it was for Mankind's Destiny.

But he was weary of wielding the sword. It was less than a month till Election Day, and he prayed devoutly that his party would be turned out of office. It was no way for a loyal party hack to be thinking, but Mulholland didn't care. It would be an admission of weakness to resign. An electoral defeat would get him out of the job much more gracefully.

CHAPTER TWO

There had been rain over Ohio during the night. For once, it had been natural rain. The weather control people engineered the weather with great care during the summer, when thirsty fields cried out for rain, and in the winter, when unchecked snow might throttle civilization. But in October the fields lay empty. There was no need for artificial rain. The rain that fell in the early hours of morning over central Ohio was God's rain, not man's, sent by the cold front sweeping southward out of Canada.

In his furnished room just off Eleventh Avenue, not very far from the university, Mike Dawes pulled the covers up over his head, retreating symbolically to the womb in hope of finding warmth and security. But it was no good. He was half awake, awake enough to realize he was awake, but still too drowsy to want to get out of bed. He could hear the pattering of the rain. It was a dark morning.

The lumo-dial of his clock read 0800 hours. He knew it was time to get out of bed. This was Wednesday, his busiest day of the academic week. At 0900 there was old Shepperd's Zoology lecture, and German at 1000 hours. *And I forgot to review those verbs,* Mike Dawes thought in irritation. *If Klaus calls on me, I'm sunk.*

He thought about getting out of bed for a few minutes; finally, he rationed himself to sixty more seconds of warmth. Counting off *a-thousand-one, a-thousand-two,* he sprang out of bed faithfully on the count of *a-thousand-*

sixty, and shivered in the bleak morning coldness.

Routine took hold of him. He stripped off his pajamas and tossed them onto the bed; he groped for a towel and his robe, found them, and made his way down the hall to the shower. He spent three minutes under the cold spray. When he returned to his room, the clock said 0813 hours. Dawes smiled. He was right on schedule. If only he hadn't forgotten about those verbs! But it was too late to fret about that. He'd have to hope for the best.

It looked as though this semester was going to be one long dreary grind, he thought as he pulled clothes from the rickety old dresser and started to climb into them. He was twenty; this was his third year at Ohio State. If all went well, he would graduate the following year and move on to medical school for four years.

If all went well.

At 0821 hours he was ready to leave: teeth brushed, hair combed, shirt buttoned, shoelaces tied. The books he would need for his morning classes were waiting on the edge of the dresser. He would have time for some orange juice, toast, and coffee at the Student Union. The probability of a surprise Zoo quiz was too great to allow for skipping breakfast; he needed all the energy he could muster. He was skinny, in the first place, stretching one hundred and fifty pounds out for six feet and an inch. In the second place, he liked to have breakfast.

Dawes started downstairs. It was still raining slightly, but not hard enough to be troublesome. Anyway, it was only a four-block walk from the rooming house where he lived to the Union.

First, though, came one particularly unpleasant morning ritual. He stopped downstairs in the hallway, where the mailboxes were. The mail was usually delivered at 0800 hours, and nobody in the house could relax until it had come. Dawes scanned the boxes as he came down the stairs. Yes, there was mail in his box. He could see the single letter leaning slantwise through the metal grill-work.

A letter from his parents in Cincinnati, maybe. Or a bill from the laundry. Or an announcement of some new show being performed by a campus group. The letter might be anything, anything at all. And he would have to go through this same little ritual of fear every morning for, perhaps, the next twenty years, until he was forty and no longer needed to worry.

His hand quivered a little as he pressed his thumb against the opener-plate. The scanner recorded his print and obediently opened the mailbox. He took out the letter.

It was a blue envelope, longer than usual, with an official penalty-for-private-use imprint where the stamp was supposed to be. Dawes' eyes travelled over the return address almost casually. *Colonization Bureau, District Board Number One, New York.*

His stomach felt queasy as he ripped the envelope hastily open.

It was addressed to him, all right. The letter, typed neatly in dark red on the standard blue paper, came quickly to the point.

You have been selected to be a member of the colonizing expedition departing on 17 October from Bangor, Maine, aboard the starship GEGENSCHEIN. You must report at once to your nearest Colonization Bureau registry center. You are now subject to the provisions of the Interstellar Colonization Act of 2099, and any violation of these provisions will meet with severe punishment.

By order of L. L. Mulholland, District Chairman.

Mike Dawes read the contents of the slip of blue paper

four times, one time after another, and with each reading the numbness grew in him. He was finding it hard to believe that he had really been called. After all, the chance was one in thousands, he thought. Why, in all his life he had only known two or three people to be called. There had been Mr. Cutley, who ran the grocery store, and Teddy Nathan, who lived on the next block. And Judy Wellington also, Dawes thought.

And now me.

'Dammit, it isn't fair!' he muttered.

'What isn't?' a casual voice asked behind him.

Dawes turned. He saw Lon Rybeck there – a senior who lived on the first floor. Rybeck still wore a dressing gown; he had no early classes, but came out to look at the mail anyway.

Mutely Dawes held up the blue slip. Rybeck's eyes narrowed and his tongue flicked briefly across his lips. 'They picked you?' he said hoarsely.

Dawes nodded. 'It just came. I have to report to the nearest registry center right away.'

'That's a lousy break, Dawes!'

'Damn right it is! Why'd they have to grab me? I'm only twenty! I haven't even finished college! I—'

He quit, realizing that he sounded foolish. Rybeck was trying to look sympathetic, but behind the expression of concern was a deeper amusement – and relief. Probability dictated that the invisible hand would not reach into this house a second time; Dawes' selection meant Rybeck could breathe more freely.

'It's rough,' Rybeck said gently. 'The morning mail comes and all your plans explode like bubbles. Where are they sending you, do you know?'

Dawes shook his head. 'It just says I'll be leaving next Wednesday from the Bangor starfield. Doesn't give the destination.'

Suddenly he did not want to talk to Rybeck any more. He had envied the older man long enough. Rybeck had a casual attitude toward grades, toward professors, toward other people, that the more conscientious Dawes had never fully understood. And now there was Rybeck, smiling ironically, standing there in his dressing gown with his life still intact. Dawes felt intolerable jealousy. He rushed past Rybeck, up the stairs and into his room.

The clock said 0830, but it didn't matter now. Dawes tossed his textbooks carelessly into the bookshelf. Nothing mattered any more. There would be no more classes for him, no more hours of study, no more ambitions. He didn't have to worry about applying to medical school. Instead of the years of study, interning and residency, struggling to set up a practice, he would live out the rest of his days on some alien world of another star.

Of all the lousy luck, Dawes thought.

He tried to rationalize it. He tried to tell himself that it was better his number had come up now, when he was still young. Except for his parents, no one would miss him very greatly. It might have been much worse if he had hung on another ten years. He visualized himself at the age of thirty, a little on the plump side, a well-fed general practitioner with a nice home in Cleveland Heights or perhaps here in Columbus. He would have a wife, two small children, a modest but growing practice. And the inexorable hand would descend and pluck him away from all that. Better to go now, he agreed bleakly.

But still better not to go at all!

He unfolded the note and read it yet again. This time he noticed the slogan across the bottom of the sheet: *Do Your Share For Mankind's Destiny.*

Twenty years ago, they had decided that mankind's destiny was in the stars. Mike Dawes had been a gurgling baby when the decision was made that, twenty years

23

hence, would rip him from the fabric of existence on Earth. Get out to the stars, that was the cry that swept newly-united Earth. Settle other worlds. Spread Earthmen through the universe. It had been a noble aim, Dawes thought. Except that nobody seemed very anxious to go. Let the *other* guy colonize the stars. Me, I'll stay here and read about it.

So there was a conscription. And now, Dawes thought, I've been caught.

. . . report at once to your nearest Colonization Bureau registry center . . .

When they said 'at once,' they meant it, Dawes knew. They meant get there within the hour. And woe betide if they discovered he had done anything to himself to make himself ineligible. There had been cases of women slashing at their bodies with knitting kneedles to disqualify themselves; naturally, only fertile colonists were wanted. But the penalty for intentional self-hurt was a lifetime at hard labor. It wasn't worth it.

Twice he reached for the phone, to call his parents in Cincinnati and let them know. Twice he drew back. They would have to be told sooner or later, he knew. But he steered away from bringing the bad news himself. Then he pictured how it would be if he remained silent and let the bureau send them its official notice. He picked up the phone again.

His father answered. Mike felt a pang of regret as he heard the voice of his father, the newsstand proprietor who had scraped for years so his favorite boy could study to be a doctor.

'Yes? Who is this?'

'Dad, this is Mike.'

'Is everything all right?' said the immediately suspicious voice. 'You got our letter? You didn't run out of money so soon, did you?'

'No, Dad. I – they've—'

'Speak up, Mike. We must have a bad connection. I can hardly hear you.'

'I've been selected, Dad!'

There was a pause, a sharp indrawing of breath. Dawes heard indistinct muttering; no doubt his father had his hand over the mouthpiece and was telling his mother about it. Dawes was grateful, for the first time, that he had never been able to afford a visual attachment for the phone. Right now he did not want to see their faces.

'When did you get the notice, boy?'

'J-just now. I have to report to the registry center right away. I leave next Wednesday.'

'Next Wednesday,' his father repeated musingly.

Dawes heard his mother sobbing in the background. She cried out suddenly, 'We won't let them take him! We won't!'

'There's no helping it, Ethel,' said his father quietly. 'Boy, can you hear me?'

'Yes, Dad.'

'Report where you're supposed to. Don't do anything wrong, do you hear?'

'I won't, Dad.'

'Will we see you again?'

'I – I suppose so. At least they ought to let us say good-bye.'

'And there isn't any way you can get out of this? I mean, once they call you, you can't appeal?'

'No, Dad. Nobody can appeal.'

'Oh. I see.'

There was another long pause. Dawes waited, not knowing what to say. He felt strangely guilty, as if he were at fault somehow for having brought this sorrow upon his parents.

His father said finally, 'So long, boy. Take care of

yourself. And let us know, soon as you know anything about where you're going.'

'Sure, Dad. Tell Mom not to worry. So long.'

He hung up the phone. After a moment, he walked to the window. The rain had stopped; it was nearly nine and the slackers were hustling to get to classes on time. Out there on campus, life was going on as usual. The football coach was sweating out tactics for Saturday's game. Shepperd was clearing his throat and stepping forward to deliver his Zoology lecture, Klaus was belaboring hapless freshmen over irregular German verbs. Life went on. The world revolved serenely around the sun. But, a week from now, Mike Dawes would be no longer part of this world.

He felt a quiet, seething anger at the injustice of it. He hadn't asked to be part of Mankind's Destiny. He had no itch to conquer other worlds. He wanted to stay on Earth, marry some reasonably pretty Ohio girl, raise some reasonably normal Ohio children.

Well, that dream was over. There was nothing left for him to do now but to walk down to the registry center and hand himself in, like a wanted criminal.

He locked his room, wondering if he would ever come back here to collect his few belongings, and trotted downstairs and into the street. It seemed to him that everyone on the street turned to look at him, as if they could see the words written in scarlet on his forehead: MIKE DAWES HAS BEEN SELECTED.

The registry center was in a loft over the movie theater. Only four days ago he had taken a girl to a movie there. They had cuddled in the balcony, ignoring the film on the tridim screen, and he had necked with her and wondered about those aspects of life that were still mysteries to him.

When you were selected, he thought, you also get a

wife. They send out fifty men, fifty women. If you happen to be married already but have no children, you can accompany your spouse as a volunteer. If you're married and do have children, and your mate is selected, you stay behind to take care of the children. Unless you and your wife go to space together, you are given one of the other colonists as a mate, and any earthside relationship you may have had is considered terminated. So he would be married soon – to someone.

He took the stairs leading to the registry center two at a time. A few boys were waiting on a bench along the wall; they peered curiously at him as he came in. They had just turned nineteen, and were waiting to register.

Dawes had registered here just a year ago. Everyone had to register at the age of nineteen; if you failed to register, you were automatically selected. So he had come in and filled out the forms, and they had put him through the diagnosing machines and then given him the quick and efficient fertility test. And, a few weeks later, he had received a card telling him that he had passed. He had shrugged and put the card in his wallet, thinking that selection was something that happened to other people.

But it had happened to him. Now.

He put his blue slip down on the reception desk and the clerk looked at it, nodding. Behind him, Dawes heard the waiting boys muttering. As a selectee, he had a certain new notoriety.

'Come this way, please,' she said solemnly to him, giving him a you-are-doing-your-share-for-mankind's-destiny look. She led him into an inner office, where a tall, balding man in his late forties sat initialing some papers.

'Mr. Brewer, this is Michael Dawes, who was selected by the New York board today.'

Brewer rose and extended a hand. 'Congratulations, Dawes. Maybe you can't see it right now, but you're about to take part in mankind's greatest adventure. Thank you, Miss Donaldson.'

Miss Donaldson left. Brewer sat down again, gesturing Dawes toward a comfortable pneumochair.

'Well?' Brewer asked. 'You're sore as hell, aren't you?'

'Am I supposed to be happy?'

Brewer shrugged. 'If you *wanted* to go to the stars, you'd have volunteered. It's a rough break, youngster. How old are you?'

'Twenty.'

'You're still young enough to adjust. Some mornings I have men in their thirties come in, men with families. You'd be surprised how many of them want to blow me up. You aren't married, are you?'

'No, sir.'

'Parents?'

'They live in Cincinnati. I've phoned them already.'

'You don't figure you have any grounds for disqualification, then.'

Dawes shook his head. In a quiet voice he said, 'I can't get out of it. I'm resigned to going. But that isn't going to make me like it.'

'We assume that,' Brewer said. 'But we also assume that you won't spend all your time sulking when you ought to be colonizing. You don't sulk for long on an alien world and stay alive.' He shook his head. 'If you think *you've* got troubles, think about the last man selected in this district. Father of three children. Age thirty-nine years, eleven months, three weeks. One week to go and he'd be ineligible, but the computer picked him. He said it was a frame-up. But he went, he did.'

'Is that supposed to make me feel better?' Dawes asked.

'I don't know,' said Brewer, sighing. 'They tell me misery loves company. You probably feel awfully sorry for yourself, and I don't blame you.'

'Will I be allowed to see my parents again?'

'You can fly to Cincy this afternoon, if you like. For the next week you'll be accompanied by a bureau guard. As a precaution, you understand. Naturally, he'll give you as much privacy as you want – in case there may be a young lady you would like to pay a farewell visit to, or—'

'Just my parents,' Dawes said.

'All right. Whatever. You have seven days. Make the most of them. You'll get a full physical next door right now. Maybe you're no longer eligible.'

'Small chance of that!'

'We can always hope, eh, Mike?'

'Why do that? What do *you* care whether I go or not? Do you know what it's like to be ripped up and tossed out into space? You're over age; you're safe.'

Brewer smiled sadly. 'I don't have a good heart; I never was eligible. But that doesn't mean I don't know what you're going through now. My wife was selected ten years ago. Come with me, Mike. The doctor will have a look at you.'

CHAPTER THREE

Cherry Thomas came awake all at once, but reluctantly, and looked around. The apartment was a mess. Two empty bottles sat on the floor near the bed, cigarette ashes were sprinkled everywhere. It had been a pleasant evening and it was good to know that somebody enjoyed your company, Cherry thought.

She lugged the cleanall out of the closet, plugged it in, and set it to work gobbling up the scattered ashes while she herself showered. The gentle cleansing spray felt good. After ten minutes under the water she stepped out, stretched, yawned, did her calisthenics. Mustn't let the middle start to sag, dearie. You're only as good as your figure is.

Morning duties over, Cherry flipped the switch on the radio; music streamed into the apartment. She jabbed down on the window-opaquer and the polarity of the glass shifted, letting in the morning sunlight. It looked as if New York would have another perfect day. The wall clock said 1123 hours, 10 October 2116.

She knew there wasn't much time. At 1300 she was due downtown for an audition; one of the big sensie-theaters needed usherettes. It was cheap work for a girl who had once danced and sung in the best establishments of three continents, but time moved along; she was twenty-five, no longer in the first golden bloom of youth, and these days the night club managers seemed to have a cradle fetish – the younger the better. Next year, Cherry thought sourly, somebody would come up with the ultimate in that line – the ten-year-old singer.

She punched out breakfast on the autocook. Cherry's apartment was automatic in almost every respect. She had always dreamed of living surrounded by the latest gadgets, and, one year when she'd really been taking in the cash, she had bought herself all the gadgets there were. An automatic backscratcher that came out of the bed's headboard when she wanted it, an autocook, automatically opaquing windows, light-dimmers, a cleanall. Her apartment was a nest for electronic wizardry of all kinds.

Cherry ate without interest. Breakfast was just something that had to be eaten, not any source of pleasure. She was tense about the audition at 1300. An usherette had to prance up and down the aisles in nothing more than a bit of hip-length, translucent fluff. She was sure she had the figure for the job, but her confidence was low. In the past year she had been gaining weight, slowly, inexorably, unstoppably.

It wasn't like this when Dan was here, she thought.

Dan had been the world to her: manager, trainer, coach, father-confessor, agent. Dan had found her when she was a dime-a-dance girl in Philadelphia, and before Dan had finished with her she was the toast of Las Vegas, Paris, Bucharest. Dan had slimmed her down, taught her poise, forced her to fight temptations, found her the best jobs and compelled her to turn down everything but the *very* best.

But Dan was gone. They had selected him, two years ago. And nothing had been the same since.

Without him she could not fend for herself. Within a year Cherry Thomas was no longer a name to put in lights; she was back singing in the dives, the flashy but tawdry joints on the wrong side of town. The big wheel had spun and the pointer had pointed at Dan, and they had taken him away and sent him out to some brand new world to build a civilization. She had wept and raged for two days, and then she drank for three more, but nothing brought him back.

Selection. The word was the foulest in Cherry's vocabulary. When someone said it in her hearing, her eyes slitted, her jaws tightened, her stomach contracted in anger and pain. Selection was a dirty word. And the man who had invented selection, whoever he was, would rot in Hell if Cherry Thomas' muttered curses could put him there.

And the worst of it was, Cherry thought, rubbing the old wound with salt for the millionth time, that she could have gone with him, if she had wanted to. 'You can always become a volunteer,' Dan had told her as she wept hysterically that morning. 'You can come with me wherever I'm going, if it means that much to you.' And he had knotted his hands in his thick dark hair and waited for her answer, and she had refused to say anything.

Well, what the hell would you do? she demanded fiercely of nobody in particular. She had been twenty-three, rolling in money, the toast of the entertainment world. He was ten years older than she. Sure, she had thought she loved him, but how can anyone be sure of that? It seemed like so much to ask, for her to give up her limousine and her apartment and her pet ocelot and her cozy, luxurious, pampered life to follow him out to the stars.

So she had finally said no, she would stay here, and Dan had shrugged calmly, telling her that it was better that way, that she was probably not fitted for the rugged frontier life anyway. And he had gone, leaving her behind. And then the anguish began for her in earnest.

She had sold the fancy cars and given away the ocelot. She still had the apartment but very little else. She had lost her cozy, luxurious life, and she had lost Dan. There had been the quick, crazy, bad marriage right after Dan was taken, a marriage that lasted only a couple of months, and after that the long, slow, gentle slide downward. The slide hadn't ended yet. Soon she'd be performing for ten bucks a night. And she would drift wearily on into her thirties and forties and maybe her fifties, growing heavier and lonelier, while Dan built log cabins in the stars. Perhaps he was dead now. What did it matter? If she had chosen to go with him, everything would have been much different.

But I was selfish. I stayed behind. And what did I get for it?

Cherry shook her head sadly, put her coffee cup into the autowash, and took a cheeriup pill from the medicine cabinet. The pill took effect practically at once: a fine, false buoyant feeling of optimism and good cheer replaced the introspective mood of gloom. She punched the dial three more times and three more little yellow pills popped out. One every four hours would see her through the day without a moment of depression; maybe the good mood was phony, but it was better than brooding about Dan all day.

She hung up her robe and eyed herself critically in the elaborate three hundred degree full-length mirror, something she never dared to do before taking her cheeriup. Fortified, she could observe her body without fear. She nodded approvingly. A visit to the steam bath, she thought, was in order, to shave a bit of poundage off the rear end. Otherwise, she was satisfied. Her belly was still flat, her bosom high and firm. She grinned at herself. That usherette's job wouldn't present any problems at all.

She dialed the wardrobe control for her clothes, and slipped rapidly into them – a one-piece blue dress with scanties underneath. No sense dressing elaborately for this kind of audition, she thought. The wardrobe indicator had already sampled the outdoor weather and reported that it was coolish; it proffered a wrap for her, and she took it.

One last check in the mirror: makeup was okay, hair well groomed, face scrubbed. Thanks to the cheeriup, she looked happy, enthusiastic, eager. The auditioners would never be able to see the core of misery deep beneath the surface.

'Good morning, Miss Thomas,' said the elevator's voice as she stepped in. A photoscanner in the elevator's roof was rigged to recognize all of the building's tenants and give them a personal greeting.

'Good morning,' she said. 'Nice day.'

There was no reply. The elevator's brain-center was programmed only for one sentence. But she believed in returning the greeting, anyway. It was the least she could do.

The elevator deposited her in the glittering chrome-and-green-glass lobby. She started to break the photobeam that controlled the front door; then, as an afterthought, she decided to see if there had been any mail for her.

That was when she found the selection notice from the Colonization Bureau.

Mirror-bright fingernails slashed the blue envelope open. She read the message carefully, slowly; reading had never been one of her strong points. When she had gone through the brief notice the first time, she doubled back and read it again.

Yes; no doubt of it. It was a selection notice.

'Well, I'll be a – So they got me, too!'

*You have been selected to be a member of the coloniz-
ing expedition departing on 17 October from Bangor,
Maine, aboard the starship GEGENSCHEIN. You must
report at once to your nearest Colonization Bureau registry center. You are now subject to the provisions of the
Interstellar Colonization Act of 2009, and any violation of
these provisions will meet with severe punishment.*

By order of D. L. Mulholland, District Chairman.

Her first reaction was an outraged one: Who the hell
are *they* that they can grab hold of Cherry Thomas and
say that she has to go out and go to the stars? They can't
push *me* around like that!

But after the first wild flare of defiance came a quieter,
more sobering thought: Maybe it won't be so bad. I
could use a change of air. I'm not going anyplace here
on Earth. In ten years I'll be a two-bit floozie. So why
not go where they want me to go?

And then came the last thought, the clincher: Maybe
you can pick the place where you're going! Maybe I can
go to the planet where Dan is!

She hurried upstairs. According to the notice, she had
to report to the nearest registry center at once. The phone
directory told her that there was a center ten blocks
away. To blazes with that audition! For the first time in
two years she felt genuine enthusiasm.

She took a cab to the registry center – no need to
worry about economizing now. She practically ran up the
stairs and into the big office. A receptionist blinked at her
and Cherry shoved the blue slip forward.

'Here. I just got this. I've been selected. Where do I
go?'

'I'll take you to the director.'

The director was a blank-faced man in his fifties who
turned on a smile when Cherry entered. She said at once,

35

'I'm Cherry Thomas. I just got selected.'

'Won't you have a seat? I'm Mr. Stewart. I realize this day is an unhappy one for you, but may I assure you—'

She cut him off. 'Look, Mr. Stewart, I want you to do me a favor. I don't mind getting selected, I suppose. But I want you to send me to the same planet where they sent Dan Cirillo in 2114. I don't know the name of the planet, but you ought to be able to look it up somewhere, and—'

Mr. Stewart's blank moon-face was furrowed by a frown. 'You don't seem to understand, Miss Thomas. You're not being sent to a planet that's already been colonized. You'll be going to a completely untamed world, a virgin planet.'

'But I want to be near Dan! Listen, he was everything to me, we were practically getting married, and then you came along and selected him. So he went out there. Well, now it's my turn, and I want to go to him! Can't you see how important it is? Damn it, don't you have any heart?'

Mr. Stewart shrugged gently. 'I'm afraid it's utterly impossible for you to follow him now. For one thing, don't you see that he's been married up there for two years?'

'Dan – married?' Cherry shook her head. *Stupid of me not to think of that! Of course, when they send you up there you have to be coupled off!* Slowly her fluttering nervous system calmed. 'I – hadn't figured on that,' she said in a soft voice. 'Sure. He got married up there.' She felt a lump sprouting at the base of her throat.

Mr. Stewart leaned forward, smiling now. 'So you see, we couldn't send you to him. Not now.'

'But I could have gone two years ago! All I had to do was come here and say the word, and you would have sent me! And I'd be up there with him now! I'd be his wife!' Her voice reached a pitch of near hysteria. She burst into sudden tears and put her head in her hands.

The peak of emotion passed in a moment or two. When she looked up, she saw Mr. Stewart watching her calmly, as if he went through this sort of thing every day.

'So I'm going to some other planet?' she asked quietly. 'Which one?'

'Only the higher authorities know that, Miss Thomas. Does it really matter?'

'No – no, I suppose it doesn't.'

He fussed uncomfortably with papers on his desk. 'I've sent for your records, but it'll take a little while. You didn't register at this office.'

'I registered in Philadelphia,' she said. 'Six years ago.' It seemed an eternity. And now, at last, her number had come up. In her mind's eye she pictured the Cherry Thomas of 2110, timidly filling out the registry form. Just a scared kid of nineteen, then. A lot had happened in six years.

Mr. Stewart said, 'I take it you're not currently married, Miss Thomas?'

'No, I was – a couple of years ago. Not now.'

'I see. And – and there isn't anyone who might possibly care to volunteer to accompany you?'

Cherry thought down the list of the men she knew. No, none of them had the stuff of a volunteer in them. She shook her head silently.

'May I ask your profession?' Mr. Stewart said.

'I'm – an entertainer.'

'That's a very general category. Would you care to be more specific?'

'Right now I'm sort of unemployed. I was supposed to get a tryout for a job this afternoon, but I guess that's out now. I've been a night-club singer, a dancer, and a couple of other things.'

She smiled ironically. Ever since they had taken Dan away, she had started every day by cursing selection and the men who ran it. But now that she herself was meshed in the net, she saw that selection was the thing she had waited for without knowing. It offered escape – escape from the harsh tinsel world she lived in, escape from the jeering booking agents who grudgingly paid her price now and who in a few years would bargain and haggle with her, escape from the inclosing wall of loneliness and fear.

A new world; a husband; children.

Her eyes felt misty with unaccustomed moisture. 'Look,' she said. 'I ain't appealing. You see they don't turn me down, hear?'

CHAPTER FOUR

People generally stepped to one side when they saw Ky Noonan coming toward them down the street. It was not only on account of his size; there are big men whose very size serves only to emphasize their essential innocuousness. But about Noonan there was that intangible air of authority, of quiet self-confidence, that silently admonished other people: *Better watch out and get out of my way. Ky Noonan is coming through!*

At thirty, he was just ripening into his physical prime. He was flamboyantly big, six feet four, a two hundred pounder who carried no fat. His jet-black hair swept backward in an untamed but somehow orderly mass that added seeming inches to his already impressive height. He had a voice to match his height, a heavy growling rumble that could be heard blocks away when he troubled to project it. His shoulders were broad, his legs long and sturdy, his skin tanned until it looked like fine cordovan or expensive morocco leather.

He had come to an important decision today. The decision had been a couple of years in the bud, years that he had spent hauling freight in Jamaica and policing the troubled frontier of South Africa. His police term had expired more than a month ago, and he had not put in an application for re-enlistment. He was restless on Earth. He had matured early, left an unmourned home at fourteen, held a hundred jobs in twenty countries since then.

Earth hemmed him in. The prison of the blue sky irked him. He wanted to leave.

They had let him have a tour of duty under the Venus dome in 2111, but that was not what he wanted, either. No place in the solar system suited him. In the system, a man either lived on Earth or he lived under a dome. Venus, Mars, Ganymede, Callisto, Titan, Pluto – six human settlements, plus one on Luna. But man was bound there, bound by the glimmering wall of duroplast that held away the encroaching poison from outside. He had spent his year on Venus gloweringly performing routine activities under the dome, while staring with undisguised anger at the red and green and blue and violet world outside, the world of formaldehyde and foul gases and weird waxen plants, the world where no man dared go without a breathing-suit and full shielding.

He did not need to visit the other solar system settlements to know that it would be the same. On Mars you looked out on dead red desert; on Ganymede you squinted past eye-searing white fields of snow to the giant unapproachable glory of Jupiter swelling in the sky. What good was it if, bound as you were to the need for oxygen and water, you left Earth only to be penned beneath a plastic dome?

No. The only world of the solar system that allowed a man to range freely over its surface unencumbered by apparatus for survival was Earth, and Earth no longer held any fascination for Ky Noonan. He longed for the stars.

Like everyone else, he registered for selection when he turned nineteen. At nineteen he was belligerent, bellicose, loudly warning the terrified technicians that they had better find him ineligible for selection, or else. But they had ignored his threats and passed him as being fit and fertile, and for a day or two he had stormed and raged at the intolerable invasion of his private rights that selection constituted.

And now he stood on a dingy, deteriorated street in old Baltimore on a mild October afternoon, outside an office on whose door was inscribed in golden letters, Colonization Bureau, District One. Local Board of Registry #212. A few simple words and he would place his private rights forever out of his own reach.

At the moment of decision he hung back, an act not characteristic of him. But he hesitated only a handful of moments. He had come this far; he realized that there could be no turning back now.

The office door was the old-fashioned kind, manually operated. He grasped the handle and pulled it open. He stepped inside.

A dozen teenagers, boys and girls, stood at a table to the left of the door, frowning busily over the registry questionnaire. To the right, several others stood on line, waiting to be admitted to the medical office for their physical examinations. All of them looked scared. Noonan smiled inwardly, knowing that by his action today he was permitting some frightened, reluctant little person to spend twenty-four extra hours on Earth.

He strode to the reception desk and said, clearly, so that everyone in the room could hear him, 'My name is Noonan. I want to volunteer.'

A dozen heads swivelled round to peer at him. There was a silence in the room. The receptionist muttered something automatic and conducted him inside, to an office whose door bore the label *Mr. Harness*.

Mr. Harness was a timorous-looking, clerkish, dried-out little man with a pretentiously solemn manner. He offered Noonan a chair and said, 'Do I understand that you wish to volunteer for selection?'

'You understand right.'

Mr. Harness steepled his fingers in a thoughtful way. 'We don't get many volunteers these days, as you can imagine. You're the first in more than a month.'

Noonan shrugged. 'Do I get a medal?'

Mr. Harness looked uncomfortable. 'Not exactly. But you do get certain privileges that the ordinary conscripts won't be entitled to. You're aware of that, aren't you?'

'I know that volunteers get their first pick of the women,' Noonan said bluntly. 'Maybe they get better food on the starship going out, too. But the women angle is the only privilege I'm interested in.'

'Ah – yes. Of course, Mr. – Mr.—'

'Noonan. Ky Noonan.'

The Bureau man reached for a data blank and a pen. 'We might as well get the details down, Mr. Noonan. Would you spell that first name, please?'

Noonan's lips twitched with sudden annoyance. 'Cyril. C-Y-R-I-L. Cyril Franklin Noonan. I call myself Ky.' The effete first name had been his mother's idea; he detested it, but all his official records bore that name, and he was too proud a man to apply for an authorized legal name-change. He called himself Ky, and let it go at that.

'Date of birth?'

'Fourth of January 2086.'

'Making you – ah – thirty. Your occupation, please?'

'Most recently, I was a policeman. A lot of other things before that.'

'Any special training? Medicine, the law, science, engineering?'

'I know how to use these—' Noonan held out his big hands – 'and I know how to use this.' He touched his forehead. 'But no professional training, no.'

Harness looked up. 'May I ask why you're volunteering, Mr. Noonan? You're not required to answer of course, but for my own personal curiosity—'

Noonan smiled. A volunteer had certain special privileges, and reticence was one of them. So long as he was deemed psychologically and physiologically fit for colonization, and so long as he was not rendered ineligible by the existence of young children who would be orphaned by his volunteering, and so long as he had not committed any serious crime, he was not required to explain. But old-maidish men like Harness wanted to know all the gossip, Noonan thought.

He said, 'For your own personal curiosity, I'm volunteering because I'm tired of staying on Earth and want to try someplace else. I'm not in debt and I haven't ruined any innocent wenches lately and I'm not volunteering to escape from a dominating mother. I'm just signing up because I want to see what it's like out there.'

Harness seemed terrified by the booming outburst. He shrank back in his chair and said, 'Yes, yes, of course, Mr. Noonan. I wasn't implying – now, if you'll simply fill out the rest of this data blank—'

Noonan filled it out. The questionnaire was a standard one; it wanted to know what jobs he'd held, what special skills, if any, he had had, what diseases he had contracted, what relatives, if any, there were. He listed as many of his jobs as he could remember, drew a casual X through the column of diseases none of which he had ever had, and left a question mark in the next-of-kin column. His parents were probably still alive, and for all he knew still living in West Virginia, but he hadn't been in touch with them for fifteen years and didn't see any point in doing it now.

He turned the blank over and found himself being asked whether he had ever been pregnant and whether he had ever had certain specific feminine complaints.

Noonan looked up. 'You sure you gave me the right form to fill out?'

Harness managed a faint grin. 'We use the same form for both sexes. Ignore the sections that aren't relevant, and go on.'

Noonan went on. When it came to the section that asked. *How much time will you need to settle your affairs?*, he wrote in impressive capitals, NONE. Signing the sheet, he handed it back to Harness, who skimmed through it and lifted his eyebrows prissily when he came to the final entry.

'You're willing to leave immediately, Mr. Noonan?'

'Why not? My affairs are in order. I don't have much property and I don't have much money, and I don't have anybody to give it to. So I'll just hand over everything I own to charity. I won't be needing money where I'm going.'

'Very well,' Harness said crisply. 'Today is October eighth. Will you report back here in three days?'

'Three days? Why?'

'According to law, you have three days to reconsider your decision. If you still want to volunteer at the end of the week, come back here and we'll finish processing your application.'

Noonan shook his head. 'I ain't gonna do any reconsidering. I made my mind up before I came in here.'

'The law prescribes—'

'To hell with the law. I came here to sign up now, not three days from now. Three days from now I want to be out of here. You get me?'

Harness looked flustered and upset, as if this deviation from accustomed routine had left him hopelessly confused and bewildered. 'Well – it's irregular, but I suppose we can waive the waiting period—'

''Yeah. Waive it.'

'Just one moment, Mr. Noonan.'

Harness swivelled around and pulled a thick leather-bound book from a shelf. He thumbed through it for several minutes while Noonan watched with mounting impatience, inwardly cursing the maddening network of regulation and ordinance that bureaucrats could weave around a man who simply wanted to join up and get moving.

Finally Harness looked up and said, 'You're in luck, it seems. The waiting period is a privilege, not a mandatory regulation. It can be waived.'

'Okay. Waive it. When do I leave?'

Order restored, Mr. Harness steepled his fingers again, carefully aligning thumb against thumb, index finger against index finger, and along down until his pinkies touched. 'It may still take a while, I'm afraid. The first thing to do is to send you next door for a medical and psychological checkup. Lord knows you *look* healthy enough, but one never can tell, can one?'

He seemed to be waiting for Noonan to agree with the platitude before he went on. Noonan remained silent. After a hesitant moment Mr. Harness continued, 'If you pass your tests this afternoon, we'll forward your papers to the Board One headquarters in New York, and you'll be included in the next list to be made up. After you're assigned to a ship, there's a wait of seven days before blastoff. No matter how impatient you are to leave, there's no getting around that seven-day wait.'

'While you check up on me and make sure I'm not skipping out on a jail term or something like that.'

Mr. Harness looked uncomfortable. 'The seven-day wait is mandatory, Mr. Noonan. You must know, certainly, that we have a certain amount of screening to do.'

'There's where you're wrong, Harness. If Earth is in such a sweat to send people out to the stars, how come nobody has ever thought of giving condemned criminals a chance to go to a colony instead of rotting in jail? You wouldn't have to let the convicts go mixed in with ordinary people; you could wait until you had an entire cargo of criminals, and send them off to some world together.'

Mr. Harness smiled coldly. 'And populate a world entirely with murderers, rapists, and thieves? I'm afraid such a colony wouldn't survive very long.'

'You know damn well it would,' Noonan said. 'They'd learn to live with each other. They'd *have* to. What you people are really afraid of is sending out a bunch of ruthless people with guts and letting them settle on a planet. You know that in a thousand years or so that world would be running the galaxy, eh, Harness?'

'I don't see what this has to do—'

'Okay. I'm just telling you. Getting an idea off my mind. Sorry I brought the whole thing up.'

Mr. Harness moistened his lips nervously. 'I fear I've no control over the policies of the Colonization Bureau in any event, Mr. Noonan. Now, if you'll step next door to the medical office—'

The medical exam went about as Noonan had expected; they gave him a thorough going-over and decided that he was in perfect health, which he could have told them in the first place. While he waited for the results of his fertility test to come from the lab, Noonan took the psych examination, which consisted of a few meaningless ink-blot and word association tests, and a short conversation designed to discover whether or not Noonan had any severe anti-social or non-cooperative tendencies.

After twenty minutes, the psychiatrist said, 'I think you'll do, Mr. Noonan. You're a stubborn man and you're a self-centered one, but you've got the stuff we need in the colonies. Suppose we check and see how your tests came out, now.'

The tests had been positive. Noonan left the registry center with a certificate of acceptance in his pocket. He had turned down the $100 bonus given to all volunteers to spend on a last-minute binge; he explained to Harness that he had more than enough money of his own to burn up in his remaining week on Earth. On his way out, he smiled at the terrified teenagers waiting in line to register. With half the world living in daily dread of the computer, it was a clean, good feeling to know that you were different, that you had walked into a registry center and told them to sign you up.

His papers were on their way by fax to New York, to the central board for this district, and the next morning they would be on District Chairman Mulholland's desk when he began to fit together his selectee list for the day. The local board would notify him where and when he was supposed to report, as soon as word came back from New York.

There was absolutely no turning back now, but Noonan did not let that trouble him. Even though he had signed a waiver, he was still free to change his mind right up until a couple of days before blastoff. But he did not intend to change his mind. And once he left Earth, he would never see it again. The trip to the stars was a one-way journey. No colonist returned.

It was late in the afternoon, past five, and night was beginning to close in. Noonan knew how he planned to spend this night; it was the way he intended to spend whatever nights remained to him on Earth. A meal and a bottle.

A cold wind whistled up Fremont Avenue toward him. He walked along, collar wide, not noticing or caring.

The first faint stars began to twinkle in the blue-black sky. He grinned at them.

Take a good look, he thought. *Take a look at me, stars. My name's Ky Noonan, and soon I'm going to be up there with you!*

CHAPTER FIVE

'Do I really have to go next week?' Carol Herrick asked hopefully. She sat tensely rigid, back straight, knees pressed tightly together, staring across the wide uncluttered desk at the elderly man who seemed, at the moment, to have absolute control over her destiny. 'I mean, isn't there some way I can get excused from having to go?'

The colonization bureau man shook his head solemnly from side to side.

'None?' Carol asked.

'If you qualify, you have to go. That's the law, and there's no way around it.'

Even delivered as gently as they were, they were stern words. Carol fought desperately to hold back the tears. She wanted to let go, to throw herself at this man's feet, to soak his knees with her tears. How could they send her to some other world? It wasn't right, she thought. She belonged here in San Francisco, with the fog and the bridges and the Sunday afternoon strolls in Golden Gate Park, not out on some strange alien planet.

She said in a soft, confused voice. 'But – why send *me*? I don't know anything about space – about the stars. I can't even cook very well. I'm not the sort of person they want up there.'

'They want all kinds of people, child. You'll learn how to cook, to sew, to skin wild animals. Space will turn you into a regular pioneer wife.'

The redness came back into her face. 'That's another thing. They're going to make me get married, aren't they? All the colonists have to marry.'

'Of course. And to bear children. We start each world with only fifty couples – but for the colony to survive, it has to multiply. Don't you want to get married, Carol? And have children?'

'Yes, I do, certainly. But—'

'But what?'

'I was waiting – waiting so long for the right one to come along. Turning down fellows, waiting to see what the next one would be like. And now it's too late, isn't it? I could have been married, maybe had a baby by now, and then I wouldn't have to go – *out there*.'

'I'm sorry. I'm supposed to give the standard speeches about Mankind's Destiny, Miss Herrick – Carol – but I suppose you wouldn't appreciate them. All I can say is, I'm sorry – but you'll have to accept your lot.'

She stared dreamily past the man behind the desk, past the banner with its meaningless slogan, past the wall itself into a gray void. She said half to herself, 'I waited so long – and now they'll marry me to the first one who comes along. Won't they?'

'There's a certain amount of choice, Carol. You're not required to accept if you don't like the man who selects you, you know. You can say no.'

'But I'll have to marry *one* of them. I can't say no to all of them.'

'Yes. You'll have to marry one of them.'

Carol shut her red-rimmed eyes for an instant, thinking of what it would be like to be married, to share a bed with a man, to feel your body swelling up with a child inside it. The idea was as strange to her as the entire notion of going to a far-off star was.

After a moment she looked up, her eyes meeting those

of the Colonization Bureau man. He looked something like her father, she thought: wise, and kind, with white hair and soft, smiling eyes – and also, like her father, behind the outward gentleness lay an inner inflexibility, an unbreakable wall of *thou must* and *thou shalt not*.

'Why?' she whispered. 'Why must I go out there? Can you tell me?'

'I can tell you, but I don't know if I can make you understand. Have you ever looked up at the sky at night and seen the stars, Carol?'

'Of course.'

'But you haven't seen all the stars. You don't see more than a few thousand stars when you look at the night sky. You may think you see millions, but you only see a handful. But there *are* millions out there, Carol. Billions. And each one of them a sun like our sun. There are hundreds of millions of solar systems in the sky. Millions of planets like Earth, where human beings can live. And it's mankind's destiny to spread out through the universe, populating those worlds. Remember, in the Bible, the Lord talking to Abraham: *"And I will make thy seed as the dust of the earth, so that if a man can number the dust of the earth, then shall thy seed also be numbered."* And then He said, *"Look now toward heaven, and tell the stars, if thou be able to number them: and so shall thy seed be."* Millions of worlds, Carol – and it's given to you to help carry the seed of Earth to the stars.'

The girl shrugged blankly. 'But why do we *have* to go to the stars? Why can't we just stay here on Earth? I don't understand why people have to be selected and sent out there. I don't want to go!'

'You'll have to go, Carol. whether you want to or not. For the destiny of mankind. Big words, words you may never understand. But you'll have to go.'

Dumbly, Carol let herself be put through the examination, unprotestingly, understanding little, filled with a vague regret and with the mild resentment that was the only anger she was really capable of.

Carol Herrick had never really given much thought to the entire immense question of selection. Three years ago, on her nineteenth birthday, she had gone downtown to this registry center, because the law required her to. She had given her name, and the doctors had examined her – that part she hadn't liked very much, walking around in underclothes while doctors asked her questions and pressed shethoscopes against her skin, even though the doctors didn't seem to regard her as anything more than a walking piece of furniture – and a week or so later she had received the little card telling her that she had qualified, that her name was on file with the big computer and that she was subject to selection until she turned forty.

She had figured out on a scrap of paper that she would not be forty until 2134, and that was so ridiculously far in the future that she could hardly visualize the stretch of years that lay between. So, because her mind could deal neither with the concept of selection nor with an interval of twenty years, she simply forgot the entire matter. She was subject to selection, she knew. Well, what of it? So was practically everybody else, and hardly anyone actually got taken, really. She knew of only one or two persons who had been selected, though she admitted that her memory didn't go back too far, that there might have been others taken when she was a little girl. She remembered the celebration there had been a few years ago, five or six, when her father had reached his fortieth birthday and was no longer eligible for selection. There had been champagne, and cigars, and they had let her have some champagne because she was seventeen and old enough to do what grownups did. But she had been sick, and thrown up in the bathroom, and after that she had gone to bed early, missing all the real fun of the party.

Selection had been something not to think about, something shadowy and unpleasant, like Death – and what normal person gave much thought to dying? Carol went through her daily routine without letting selection color her life. She was graduated from high school and found a job in Oakland, as a secretary in a big construction firm, and every day she took the bus through the tube under the bay, and did her day's work, and came home and watched television and went out on a date or went to bed early.

Only now all that was finished. The little blue slip in the mailbox had finished all that.

Carol had left for work at the usual time that day, and as usual she had not bothered to check the mailbox on her way out – if she got a letter as often as once a month, that was unusual. But when she reached her office, at 0900, there was a message waiting on her desk.

Your mother called. Wants you to call her back when you come in. Urgent.

And Carol had punched out the number and waited trembling for the call to flash across the bay to San Francisco, and her mother's face had come on the screen pale and tear-streaked. For a moment her mother had not been able to speak, and Carol thought dully that Daddy must have died. But then the words came out in a tumbling rush: *'Carol baby, we got the notice, you've been selected!'*

Selected. Carol had smiled; selection was something that happened to other people. But it had happened to her. Other people in the office had heard her mother's words as they came blurting over the phone; the news spread, and as the gloomy-faced fellow workers gathered round to mutter little speeches of commiseration, Carol began to realize that being selected was very serious indeed.

They had let her go home from the office right away, and she had ridden back across the bay; her mother was having hysterics and her father, summoned home from work, sat grimly staring at a half-empty liquor bottle, and her twelve-year-old brother, white-faced and confused, looked at her strangely and said nothing. That was what being selected was like, she thought. It was like dying, only you stayed around for a little while after you had died, and watched the way the survivors mourned you.

She had reported to the registry center as required, and they had shown her to the kindly-looking man who was in charge, and she had tried to explain that the stars held no interest for her, that she was just an ordinary office girl with no desire to be a pioneer, that she did not want to go to space.

But her wishes, it seemed, did not matter. There was no way out. The blue slip of paper with its neat red typing said, *You have been selected to be a member of the colonizing expedition departing on 17 October from Bangor, Maine, aboard the starship GEGENSCHEIN.* It was a government order, and there could be no argument. In only a week, she would be bound for the stars.

When she had first registered, they had given her a little blue-covered booklet that explained how selection worked and what colonization was like. She had read it through and thrown it away, finding it of no great importance. Now she asked for and was given another copy, and after her re-examination she sat in an empty anteroom waiting for the verdict, reading the booklet they had given her.

She skipped through the parts about how selection

worked, the central computer and the local boards and the five districts and all the rest. That part of it no longer concerned her, not now. Turning to the part that told of how a colony operated, she read carefully, looking at each word before moving on to the next.

They picked out a hundred people, fifty men and fifty women, and sent them off to a planet in the sky. Along with them went tools and books and medical supplies and whatever else a brand new world needed. One of the hundred colonists was chosen as the colony director, and he served until the colonists decided to elect somebody else.

The first thing they did was to marry everybody off. Colonists had to be married and were supposed to have as many children as they could. The way it worked, all the unmarried people of the colony divided up, men and women, and then the men picked, in a special order. The women could accept or refuse, as they liked, but at the end everyone had to be married to someone, and if a woman refused everyone the colony director was entitled to assign a husband for her.

Carol put down the booklet, frowning. The idea of being married was a little frightening. She remembered the day of her eighteenth birthday, and her mother saying, 'Well, Carol, now you're eighteen. You'll be a married woman before you know it!'

Four years ago. And in the time since, her mother had brought the subject of marriage up time and again. Certainly there had been plenty of candidates. The first boy who had wanted to marry her was Phil, and she might have said yes to him, but she didn't really like him enough.

After him, there had been that tall boy, Tom. Tom might have been all right, but he wanted to write poetry, and what future did a girl have married to a poet? And after Tom—

After Tom there had been Paul, but Paul was old, almost thirty, and he was getting bald and fat around the middle; she had said no to Paul. After Paul, Richard; after Richard, Dave. No to Richard, no to Dave. Carol had kept waiting, waiting, as her twentieth year ended and her twenty-first began, and then as that year came round to its finish. Why marry now? There was always the hope that Prince Charming would come riding up in his glossy brand-new Frontenac limousine and sweep her off her feet.

So she had waited for that one perfect mate, for the husband that heaven had set aside for her alone, and in the meantime the wheel had turned and selection had taken her instead. Now, faced for the first time with a major crisis, Carol took a rare introspective glance and realized, with mild shock, that perhaps she had not wanted to marry at all. Perhaps she had been fooling everyone, herself, and her parents and her succession of beaux, into thinking she was shopping for a mate when actually all she wanted was to remain at home, with Mother and Dad and brother, in her own clean little room, alone in the bed she had slept in since childhood, calm, untroubled by the confusions that marriage undoubtedly would bring.

A strange realization. Am I really like that, she wondered? And then she corrected herself: *Was* I really like that? The Carol Herrick who had been existed no more. No longer did she have any control over what happened to her.

Now they would take her away from her home and her parents and the old black teddy-bear on the dresser, and send her to a strange place and push her into the arms of a strange man. Funny, she thought: right now the man who is going to be my husband is sitting in a registry center, cursing and complaining, waiting to find out if he will be declared eligible. What will he be like? He could be as old as forty, she knew. Almost as old as her father. That would be odd, being married to a man that old.

Or, perhaps, her husband might be nineteen or twenty, a frightened boy. That might not be so dreadful: she could be a sort of older sister or aunt to him, as well as a wife. Calm his fears, and in that way ease her own.

But anyone at all might pick her. A burly truck driver, brutal and selfish; a wispy little college professor; a coarse, ugly man like the fisherman she had seen at the wharf, with a twisted nose and the reek of prawns about him.

She closed the booklet. A banner on the wall commanded, *Do Your Share for Mankind's Destiny*.

Why? Why this senseless hurling out of bewildered people to the stars? Carol Herrick had no idea. Meekly, she was being swept along on the tide.

The door opened. The kindly white-haired man stood there with papers in his hand.

'Well?' Carol asked.

'The test result was positive. In other words, you're passed. You're eligible.'

Carol nodded slowly. 'I have to go, then.'

'Yes. You have to go.'

In the empty room the fatal words echoed resonantly like a sentence of death. Carol took an uncertain step forward. She was going to the stars. Uncomplainingly and uncomprehendingly, she was going to do her share for Mankind's Destiny.

CHAPTER SIX

After completing his list of one hundred ten names for the seventeenth of October blasting of the *Gegenschein*, District Chairman Mulholland turned his attention to the next item on his daily routine: finalization, as they so barbarously called it in scheduling, of the previous day's list.

The October 16 ship was the *Skyrover*, departing from the Cape Canaveral base. Mulholland had prepared the usual quota of names; during the early hours of the morning, while he had been assembling the *Gegenschein* list, word was coming in from the local boards on the previous day's selections. Mulholland scanned the long yellow sheets. The *Skyrover* list would present no difficulties, he saw. There were fifty-one elegible males, fifty-two eligible women.

He deleted the three surplus names, entered them on the proper form, and gave the deletion list to Miss Thorne. During the day three people somewhere in the United States would learn that they had received a minute's reprieve; instead of departing as they had been told on the October 16 ship, they would be held over until October 17, and, if not needed to fill vacancies on the *Gegenschein* list, would certainly be included on the list of whatever ship was scheduled for departure on the 18th.

His job, Mulholland thought, was like a kind of cosmic jigsaw puzzle – a puzzle in which he used human pieces, scooping up a hundred at a time, discarding those which might be bent or broken and unsuitable for the pattern, fitting the rest into place. Each day another pattern had to be created; sometimes there were too many pieces, and some were put aside for another day.

He completed the *Skyrover* list and sent it down the pneumotube to Brevoort, twenty storeys below. Brevoort would phone Cape Canaveral and advise them verbally of the completion of the list; the list itself would be sent to Florida by fax at the same time. With the *Skyrover* under control, Mulholland was finished for the day. The time was 1400 hours. At the Bangor starfield that moment, the *Enterprise Three* was blasting off, with one hundred colonists aboard, people who had been selected a week before.

It went on constantly, day and night – people registering for selection, people being selected, people reporting for blastoff, ships departing. Five ships leaving a day from the United States alone, sixty from the world, four hundred twenty ships a week. And, so immense were the heavens, it would be untold centuries before the last habitable planet had been colonized by men of Earth.

1400 hours. The end of the day. Mulholland tidied his desk and said his goodbyes – most of the clerical workers had two hours before their day ended – and left. As he stepped outside, into the bracing October wind, he tried to shrug off his day's labor like an otter coming to shore and shaking itself dry. Once 1400 hours came, he could stop being District Chairman Mulholland, wielder of the sacred staff; he could go back to being plain Dave Mulholland of White Plains. Once aboard the sleek bullet of a train, he smiled politely to other commuters whose faces if not names he knew, and settled back in his padded seat. The nonstop White Plains express made the trip in seven minutes. Years ago, before the new trains had been put in use, the trip took longer, long enough for him to have a drink and relax before arriving at the White Plains station. But there was no time for a drink now.

One was waiting for him at home, though, an icy martini. Mulholland kissed his wife, patted the bouncingly joyful dog, drank his drink.

'Anything new, dear?' Ellen asked. She was forty-one; safe from selection, at last. Like him, her hair was red – 'You're bound to raise a flock of redheads,' friends had said over and over, when they were married sixteen years before. But they had no children. Out of fear of selection, perhaps, Mulholland admitted.

'Nothing new, Ellen. The same as always. One hundred heads on the block.'

She looked at him painfully, but kept unsaid what she was thinking. They had been over the same ground often enough in the past. The job was tearing him apart - nobody loves the public executioner or the baseball umpire or the local boss of selection – but resignation was impossible. You didn't toss away a job the party had carefully gained for you. If you did, there would be no further jobs forthcoming from them – ever.

Mulholland changed into his puttering clothes. There was work to do in the garden, in what remained of the afternoon. He enjoyed working with his hands, grubbing down in the dirt to bed an azalea or trim a privet hedge. He could get absorbed in the mere physicality of the work, absorbed enough to forget that a hundred people in the United States were cursing him bitterly because he had done the job he was paid to do.

At least, he thought, it wasn't so bad now that he didn't have to hear appeals. He sat in lofty isolation in his office, drawing up lists and initialing forms; at least he had no direct contact with the victims he was condemning. Before reaching the top, when *he* had been one of the subchiefs in charge of refusing appeals, the job had been infinitely more painful.

He remembered some of the appeals. There was the poet embarked on an immense verse cycle, who arrived bearing a petition from some of the world's leading creative figures begging that he be excused in the name of culture. The poet had been shipped out with regrets; the surest way to destroy selection would be to begin making exceptions in the name of minority interests. Then there had been countless parents who could not bear separation from their children or from each other; students who pleaded for a chance (denied) to complete their educations; stage figures asking (unsuccessfully) to be allowed to finish the runs of their plays. Selection could make no exceptions. Whatever the cost to Earth in terms of a work of poetry forever lost, a hit play closed, a potential Einstein shipped to the stars, such losses had to be endured. To permit creative people, people of genius, to escape the net of selection would be to insure that only mediocrities would go to the stars, and mankind's destiny thus would be thwarted.

Mulholland finished his garden work, went indoors, washed, had another cocktail, ate dinner. In the evening, several hours of reading, a bit of music, an hour or two of video, a sedative, and bed.

He had few personal friends these days. Once he had been more gregarious, but nowadays social relationships were difficult for him to maintain. Either people regarded him with thinly veiled horror (who wants to play bridge with the hangman?) or else they cultivated his friendship with the hope that someday he might do them a favor, when selection struck their home. Of course, he could do no favors, but people never seemed to believe that.

He went to bed at 2300 hours. He was up again at 0730,

shaved and showered and dressed and fed within forty-five minutes. On his way to the station he saw a mail truck making its rounds with the morning delivery, and felt little comfort from the fact that he no longer needed to dread the arrival of a blue envelope. It was impossible for him ever to forget that two hundred million Americans lived in the grip of terror each morning between breakfast and the arrival of the day's mail, never knowing until the red-white-and-blue truck had made its appearance whether or not this would be the day their number came up.

At 0900 on the dot, Mulholland was at his office. The requisition form was waiting for him, as always; fifty couples were needed for the starship *Aaron Burr*, leaving Canaveral on the eighteenth of October. He went through the standard morning routine, authorizing the selection of one hundred ten names for the *Aaron Burr*.

Two hours later, the first replies began to come in from the local boards on the *Gegenschein* selectees. Mulholland put each form in the 'hold' basket and forgot about them until it was time to get back to the *Gegenschein* list. He had already forgotten about the *Skyrover*; now that its list was complete, it faded into the long blur of unremembered ships whose passengers Mulholland had authorized.

After lunch – a tense affair as always for he never digested well on a working day – he turned his attention to the *Gegenschein*. His notes told him that one slot had already been filled: Noonan, the volunteer sent through from Baltimore Board #212. Mulholland needed forty-nine men, fifty women to make up the complement.

Most of the east coast and midwest reports had come in already. The western people, naturally, would take longer; in most cases the mail was just being delivered now, out on the Coast. But there were enough early returns to begin working with. Mulholland began to sort through them, checking them off against his master file.

Columbus, Ohio Board #156 We have examined registrant Michael Dawes and find him acceptable for selection . . .

New York Board #11 We have examined registrant Cherry Thomas and find her acceptable for selection . . .

Philadelphia Board #72 We have examined registrant Lawrence T. Fowler and find him acceptable for selection . . .

And, mixed with the rest, a red slip that signified a turndown: *Atlanta Board #243 We have examined registrant Louetta Johnson and find her not acceptable for selection for the reasons detailed below. . . .*

Mulholland paused, turned the red slip over, and read it. Louetta Johnson had been found after due medical examination to be in her twelfth week of pregnancy, this fact being unknown to Miss Johnson, who therefore had not notified the registry center of this change in her status.

He put her slip aside and crossed her name from his list. Within the next hour, he lost two more of his possibles: the 93rd Board, in Troy, New York, reported that Elgin MacNamara had been the victim of a fatal auto accident the very day of his selection the 114th Board, in Elizabethtown, Kentucky, regretfully informed the District Chairman that registrant Thomas Buckley had been taken into custody after allegedly shooting his wife and another man, and would not be eligible for a berth on the *Gegenschein.*

But, despite these minor setbacks, the list slowly filled. By 1320 hours, Mulholland's tally showed forty-three men and thirty-nine women assigned to the *Gegenschein,* with five of his original hundred and ten disqualified and twenty-three yet to be heard from. Not long after that, the first reports began to come in from the far west:

San Francisco Board #326 We have examed registrant Carol Herrick and find her acceptable for selection . . .

Los Angeles Board #406 We have examined registrant Philip Haas and find him acceptable for selection . . .

A red slip from Seattle Board #360: *Registrant Ethel Pines declared ineligible on medical grounds; registrant Pines has cancer.* Mulholland removed the name of Ethel Pines from his list.

By 1340 hours, he was nearing completion. A quick check indicated that he had forty-eight men, forty-six women. Ten of his original hundred and ten were scratched, ineligible. One volunteer. Seven reports were yet to come in.

Ten minutes later, they were in: five acceptables, two rejects. Mulholland drew a line under the column of male names and quickly counted upward: fifty names in all, headed by Cyril Noonan, volunteer. He was short one woman.

Now he reached into his replacement basket and drew out the three cards that had been left over from the *Skyrover* quota. One man, two women. Mulholland put the man's card aside. He flipped the other two cards into the air. One landed face up; he snatched at it – the card of a woman named Marya Brannick.

Marya Brannick's name was entered in the fiftieth slot on the distaff side of the *Gegenschein* list. Carefully putting the completed *Gegenschein* list to one side, Mulholland took tomorrow's *Aaron Burr* list from its pigeonhole and inscribe the names of Irwin Halsey and Maribeth Jansen at the heads of the two columns.

He buzzed for Miss Thorne.

'Jessie, I've assigned the three leftovers from the *Skyrover* list. Brannick goes into the *Gegenschein*, Halsey and Jansen are being held over till tomorrow for the *Aaron Burr.*'

Miss Thorne nodded efficiently. 'I'll see that the notification goes out to the local boards. Anything else, Mr. Mulholland?'

'I don't think so. Everything's under control.'

She gave him a toothy smile and scuttled back to her adjoining cubicle. Sighing, Mulholland checked the clock. 1358 hours. Astonishing how smoothly the selection mechanism works, he thought. The list gets filled as if by clockwork.

And it *had* been clockwork, he realized, with himself doing nothing that a robot was unable to do. He wondered what a film of himself at work on a typical day would look like, speeded up a little. Even more ridiculous than the ancient fast-camera films, no doubt. He would emerge on the screen as an inane fat little bureaucrat, busily pulling lists in and out of pigeonholes, inscribing names, juggling surpluses, carrying forth extra selectees until they were needed, signing documents, self-importantly buzzing for his secretary—

It was an unflattering picture. Mulholland tried to blank it out, but the image refused to quit his mind. Thank God it was quitting time, he thought.

He studied the completed *Gegenschein* list again. It looked all right: the hundred names, fifty in each column, each on its appointed line. He skimmed down the men's list: *Noonan, Cyril; Dawes, Michael; Fowler, Lawrence; Matthews, David;* And right along to the names at the bottom: *Nolan, Sidney; Sanderson, Edward.*

He checked out the women's column next: *Thomas, Cherry; Martino, Louise; Goldstein, Erna;* And down to the last, the ink not yet dry on her name: *Brannick, Marya.*

Mulholland nodded. Fifty here, fifty there. The list was okay. He scrawled his signature in the proper place. Another day, another shipload, he thought. Another cargo for his conscience.

The long list of names wavered, blurred; he closed his tired eyes. But that was a mistake. His imagination responded by conjuring up images of people; names took on flesh, faces hovered accusingly in the air. Edward Sanderson, he thought – and pictured, for no particular reason, a short, slim, narrow-shouldered man with thinning brown hair. Erna Goldstein – she might be a dark-haired girl with large eyes, who majored in dramatics in college and had hopes of writing a play, someday. Sidney Nolan—

Mulholland shook his head to clear it. He had managed to keep this from happening all day, this sudden taking on of flesh on the part of the names on his list. So long as he thought of them simply as names, as strings of syllables, everything was all right. But once they began asserting their humanity, he crumbled beneath the assault.

Hastily he pressed his thumb against the sensitized spot, rolled up the sheet, stuffed it in its little cylinder, and sent it rocketing down the pneumotube to the waiting Brevoort. The *Gegenschein* had her cargo, barring accidents and possible suicides between now and the seventeenth of the month.

The clock said 1400 hours. The day was over. Mulholland rose, sticky with sweat, eyes aching, mind numb. He was free to go home.

At least you only get selected once, he thought. *I have to go through this every day.*

He tidied his desk and moved in a shambling way toward the door. Tomorrow, the *Aaron Burr* list would have to be finalized, and some new list would be begun.

And after that, the weekend, when Dick Brevoort moved upstairs to prepare the Saturday and Sunday lists. The wheels of selection never ceased grinding, even though an individual component of the great machine might occasionally require a couple of days of rest.

Mulholland peered into the adjoining office. Miss Thorne was behind her typewriter, spine stiff, fingers sharply arched. She seemed supremely happy in her business. Mulholland wondered if the names she typed so busily all day ever came to haunt her. Probably not, he decided. She could go home each night with a clear conscience to whatever she enjoyed doing in the evenings, crocheting or watching video or listening to sixteenth-century madrigals.

He looked in. 'Good afternoon, Jessie.'

'Good afternoon, Mr. Mulholland. Have a very pleasant evening.'

'Thanks,' he said in a suddenly hoarse voice. 'The same to you, Jessie.'

He walked slowly toward the door.

CHAPTER SEVEN

Bangor Starfield, from which three ships of colonists departed every week, covered sixteen square miles of what had once been virgin forest in northern Maine. The lofty firs were gone; now the area had been cleared and levelled and surrounded by a fence labelled at thousand-yard intervals, NO ADMITTANCE EXCEPT TO CLASSIFIED PERSONNEL. BY ORDER OF COLONIZATION BUREAU.

Within the fenced-off area there was surprisingly little in the way of construction. Since the starfield was for government use only, not commercial, there was no need for the usual array of terminals, passenger buildings, waiting rooms, and concessions that cluttered every commercial spaceport. The buildings at the Bangor field were few: a moderately elaborate barracks for the permanent staff, a more sketchily constructed housing unit for transients, a couple of staff amusement centers, and a small administration building. All these were huddled together in a compact group in the center of the cleared area. Fanning off in three directions were the blastoff fields themselves, kept widely separated because a starship likes a mile or two of headroom when it can get it.

On the morning of the seventeenth of October, 2116, two of Bangor Starfield's three blastoff areas were occupied. On Field One stood the *Andrew Johnson*, solemnly alone with a mile of heat-fused sterile brown earth on each side: a tall steel-blue needle that towered erect on its landing-jacks and retractile atmospheric fins. The *Andrew Johnson* was scheduled for departure on the twentieth of the month; tomorrow the service crews would swarm out to Field One to begin the three-day countdown that prefaced every departure of a starship.

At present the service technicians were busily running the final tests on the *Gegenschein*, which stood in the center of Field Three, slim and straight, glinting golden in the morning sunlight. The *Gegenschein* was due for blastoff at 1600 hours that afternoon, and with the countdown in its final six hours the service crews scuttled like busy insects through the ship, making certain that everything was in perfect order. Only once, twelve years before, had there been a major starship accident, but it was hoped that there would never be another.

Field Two remained empty. A returning starship, the *Wanderer*, was due back late that evening, and Field Two was being held open for it. A small service crew was on duty at the Field Two blockhouse, running final checks on the guidance system that would monitor the *Wanderer* into its landing orbit later in the day. Nothing could be left to chance – not with a hundred-million-dollar starship.

From the upper floor of the housing unit for transients, looking out past the squat yellow-brick edifice that served as the permanent staff residence barracks, both the *Andrew Johnson* and the *Gegenschein* could be seen, one at the western end of the field, the other far to the east. Mike Dawes, who had arrived at the Bangor Starfield at 0945 hours after an early-morning flight from New York, peered out the window of the small room to which he had been assigned, looking first at the distant, blue-tinted *Andrew Johnson*, then, turning eastward, at the much closer *Gegenschein*.

'Which one am I going on?' he asked.

'The gold-colored one,' said the uniformed Colonization Bureau guard who had shown him to his temporary room. 'It's on Field Three, over there.'

Dawes nodded. 'Yes. I see it.'

'You've got an hour or so to rest here and relax. At 1100 hours there's a preliminary briefing session downstairs in the central hall. You won't be able to miss it; just turn to your left when you leave the elevator. The briefing lasts about an hour. Then you'll be given lunch.'

'I'm not going to be very hungry,' Dawes said.

The guard smiled. 'Most of them never are. But the meal is always a good one.'

The condemned man ate a hearty meal, Dawes thought. He realized with a strange sense of loss that he had only one more meal to take on Earth; after that, he might never again taste the egg of a chicken or the leg of a lamb, might never again put to his lips a tomato or a cucumber or a radish. It was a small loss, but a telling one. Life on Earth was just such a confection of little details.

'What time is blastoff?' he asked.

'1600 hours. Don't worry – they'll fill you in on the schedule downstairs.'

'I suppose they will.'

'Any other questions?'

Dawes shook his head. The guard walked to the door, opened it, paused before stepping out. 'Remember,' he said. 'You can't leave this building without a pass. The best thing is simply to stay in your room until the gong rings for the briefing session.'

'I'm not going to run away,' Dawes said.

The door closed behind him.

He looked around at his room, his home for what was left of his stay on Earth. It was hardly imposing. The room was an ugly little box whose severity was lessened only by the picture window opening out onto the field. The walls were painted dull green; there was a bed, a chair, a dresser, a washstand. It looked like a five-dollar room in some cheap hotel. His one piece of luggage stood near the door. He had been allowed twenty pounds of personal effects aside from the required articles of clothing. He had chosen books, checking first as advised to make certain that none of his choices would be duplicated in the colony's filmed library.

It had been a long week, he thought, as he sank down on the chair near the window and looked out at the ship that soon would carry him to the stars. It had taken him a day or so to withdraw from the college, settle his campus debts, and pack; he had given his textbooks to the university library, handed over his pitiful college souvenirs, the usual assortment of enamelled beer-mugs and banners and beanies, to a sophomore living on the same floor at his boarding house.

Then he had returned to Cincinnati, accompanied by a watchful minion of the Colonization Bureau, for a painful and depressing final visit home. His parents were not taking his selection very well. His father, a tight-lipped man who rarely displayed any outward sign of emotion, was doing his best to show a stiff upper lip and bear up under the calamity, but it was obvious that the news was rapidly bringing him to a state of collapse. His mother had become almost totally inarticulate; all she could do was stare soulfully at her son, sniffle, sob.

His older brother had come up from Kentucky, looking peevish and fretful about the sudden intrusion of Mankind's Destiny into the Dawes family. 'Something's gotta be done about this selection business,' Dan kept repeating, rubbing his thinning scalp. 'You can't just

71

let the guvviment go around grabbing up people, a promising doctor like Mike, heave them out into space like this.'

His married sister had flown home from Tacoma with her paunchy, piously inclined husband; she sobbed over her departing brother, which annoyed Dawes because she had treated him like a slave when they were younger, while her husband mouthed consoling platitudes about fate and destiny.

It was like a wake, Dawes thought, only the guest of honor was up and around to greet everyone. He felt acutely uncomfortable during his three-day stay at his parents' home. And finally he could take the protracted goodbying no longer, and, conniving with the bureau watchdog, told them that he had to go on to New York for final briefing.

They accompanied him to the airport, wailing and weeping all the while. And then a segment of his life on Earth ended, as he said his final goodbyes to his family and climbed aboard the plane for New York.

Although he stayed in a fine hotel at bureau expense, his stay in New York was far from pleasant. The great buildings, the shows, the people, the bustling vitality – everything served only to remind him of the world he was giving up, in exchange for some lonely alien ball of mud which he was exposed to help convert into a simulacrum of Earth. He had seen so little of his own world, really. There was all of Europe: Paris, London, Bucharest, Moscow, the great cities he would never have a chance to visit now. The Orient; Africa, the Pyramids, the Nile, Japan, China; he had never even seen the Grand Canyon. And now he never would.

The two days at large in New York dragged mercilessly. He wondered how, in the old days, selectees had managed to endure three whole months of lame-duck existence on Earth; he was fearfully impatient to be gone and done with it, instead of lingering for a few final days. He was grateful when, early on the morning of the 17th, he was taken to the airport and flown to Bangor.

And now he could see the *Gegenschein* sitting on the field, in the last stages of its countdown. At 1600 hours, it was goodbye to Earth. He paced his room impatiently, waiting for the minutes to tick past.

At 1100 hours a gong sounded in the hall. A speaker in the corner of his room rang crisply, 'All selectees are to report to Room 101 for indoctrination. Place your baggage in the hall outside your room for pickup.'

Dawes left his suitcase in front of his door and followed the flickering neon signs down the hall to the elevator, and from there to Room 101. Room 101 was a huge auditorium in the center of the compound; several men in blue-and-yellow uniforms bustled about on a dais, adjusting a microphone, while pale, tense-faced civilians filtered in and took seats as far away from each other as possible.

Dawes slipped into an empty row near the back and looked around, seeing his fellow selectees for the first time. One hundred people were spread thinly about in an auditorium big enough for ten times that number. He managed an ironic smile at the way each selectee had managed to place himself on a little island, insulated by five or six empty seats on each side from his nearest neighbor, as if afraid of impinging on the final hours of anyone's privacy. They seemed to be ordinary people; Dawes noticed that most of them appeared to be in their late twenties or early thirties, and a few were older than that. He wondered whether the colonies were portioned out strictly at random, or whether perhaps some degree of external control was exerted. It was perfectly within the range of probability for the computer to select fifty men of twenty and fifty women of forty to comprise a colony, but it seemed unlikely that such a group would ever be allowed to go out.

Someone in this room is going to be my wife, Dawes thought with sudden surprise. His heart pounded tensely at the thought, and color came to his face. *Which one of them will it be?*

Behind him, the auditorium doors closed. An officer with an array of ribbons and medals on his uniform front stepped up to the dais, frowned at the microphone, raised it a fraction of an inch, and said, 'Welcome to Bangor Starfield. I'm Commander Leswick, and your welfare will be my responsibility until you blast off at 1600 hours. I know this has been a trying week for you, perhaps virtually a tragic week for some, and I don't intend to repeat the catch-phrases and slogans that you've been handed for the past seven days. You've been selected; you're going to leave Earth, and you'll never return. I put it bluntly like this because it's too late for illusion and self-deception and consolation. You've been picked for the most important job in the history of humanity, and I'm not going to pretend that you're going out on an easy assignment. You're not. You're faced with the tremendous challenge of planting a colony on an alien world trillions of miles from here. I know, right now you feel frightened and lonely and wretched. But never forget this; each and every one of you is an *Earthman*. You're a representative of the highest form of life in the known galaxy. You've got a reputation to live up to, out there. And you'll be building a world. To the future generations on that world, you'll be the George Washingtons and Thomas Jeffersons and John Hancocks.

'The planet you're going to is the ninth out of sixteen planets revolving around the star Vega. Vega is one of the brightest stars in the sky, and also one of the closest to

74

Earth – twenty-three light-years away. You're lucky in one respect: there are two colonizable planets in the Vega system, your world and the eighth planet, which is not yet settled. That means you'll eventually have a planetary neighbor, unlike most other colonies which are situated on the only habitable world in their system. The name of your planet, by the way, is Osiris, from Egyptian mythology – but you can call it anything you like, once you get there.

'The trip will take about four weeks, even by Einstein Drive. That'll allow you plenty of time to get to know each other before you reach your new planet. Captain McKenzie and his crew have made several dozen success-ful interstellar flights, and I can assure you you'll be in the best possible hands.

'The name of your ship, as you know, is the *Gegen-schein*. We draw the names of our ships from three sources: astronomical terms, historical figures, and tradi-tional ship names. *Gegenschein* is an astronomical term referring to the faint luminosity extending along the plane of the ecliptic in the direction diametrically oppo-site to the sun – the sun's reflection, actually, bouncing back from an immense cloud of stellar debris.

'I think that covers all the essential points you'll need to know at the outset. We're going to adjourn to the mess hall now for a most significant occasion – the last meal you're ever going to eat on the planet Earth, and also the first meal you will eat with each other. I hope you all have good appetites, because the meal is a special one.

'Before we go in, though, I'm going to call the roll. When you hear your name, I want you to stand up and make a complete three hundred and sixty degree revolu-tion, letting everyone get a look at you. This is as good a time as any to start getting to know each other.'

He picked up a list. 'Cyril Noonan.'

The rangy, powerful-looking man in the front row rose and said, in a booming voice that filled the auditorium easily, 'The name I use is Ky Noonan.'

Commander Leswick smiled. 'Ky Noonan, then. Incidentally, Ky Noonan happens to be a Volunteer.'

Noonan sat down. Commander Leswick said, 'Michael Dawes.'

Dawes rose, blushing unaccountably, and stood awkwardly at attention. Since he was at the back of the auditorium, there was no need for him to turn around. A hundred heads craned backward to see him, and he sat.

'Lawrence Fowler.'

A chunky man in the middle of the auditorium came to his feet, spun round, smiled nervously, and sat down. Leswick called the next name, and the next, until all fifty men had been called.

He began on the women after that. Dawes watched closely as the women rose. Most of them, he saw, were eight to ten years older than he. But he paid careful attention. There was one girl named Herrick who interested him. She was young and looked attractive, in a wide-eyed, innocent way. Carol Herrick, he thought. He wondered what she was like.

CHAPTER EIGHT

It was probably an excellent meal. Dawes did not appreciate it, though. He ate listlessly, picking at his food, unable to enjoy the white, tender turkey, the dressing and trimmings, the cold white wine. Although he had overcome his initial bitterness over selection, a lingering tension remained. He had no appetite. It was an inconvenience shared by most of his fellow selectees, evidently, judging by the way they toyed with their food.

The selectees had been distributed at ten tables. Dawes was dismayed to find, when he took his seat, that he could not recall the names of any of the other nine selectees at his table. But his embarrassment was short-lived. A roundfaced, balding man to his left said, 'I'll confess I didn't catch too many names during rollcall. Maybe we ought to introduce ourselves all over again. I'm Ed Sanderson from Milwaukee. I used to be an accountant.'

It went around the table. 'Mary Elliot, St. Louis,' said a plump woman with streaks of gray in her hair. 'Just a housewife before my number came up.'

'Phil Haas, from Los Angeles,' said a lean-faced man in his late thirties. 'I was a lawyer.'

'Louise Martino, Brooklyn,' said a dark-haired girl of twenty-five or twenty-six, in a faltering, husky voice. 'I was a salesgirl at Macy's.'

'Mike Dawes, Cincinnati. Junior at Ohio State, premed student.'

'Rina Morris, from Denver,' said a good-looking redhead. 'Department store buyer.'

'Howard Stoker, Kansas City,' rumbled a heavy-set man with a stubbled chin and thick, dirty fingers. 'Construction worker.'

'Claire Lubetkin, Pittsfield, Massachusetts.' She was a bland-faced blonde with a nervous tic under her left eye. 'Clerk in a video shop.'

'Sid Nolan, Tulsa. Electrical engineer.' He was a thin, dark-haired, fidgety man who toyed constantly with his silverware.

'Helen Chambers, Detroit,' said a tired-looking woman in her thirties, with dark rings under her eyes. 'Housewife.'

Ed Sanderson chuckled uncomfortably. 'Well, now we know everyone else, I hope. Housewives, engineer, college student, lawyer—'

'How come there ain't any rich people selected?' Howard Stoker demanded suddenly. 'They just take guys like us. The rich ones buy themselves off.'

'That isn't so,' Phil Haas objected. 'It just happens that most of the wealthy executives and industrialists don't get to be wealthy until they're past the age of selection. But don't you remember a couple of months ago, when they selected that oilman from Texas—'

'Sure,' Sid Nolan broke in. 'Dick Morrison. And none of his father's millions could get him out.'

Stoker growled something unintelligible and subsided. Conversation seemed to die away. Dawes looked down at his plate, still largely untouched. He had nothing to say to these people with whom he had been thrown by the random hand of selection. They were just people. Strangers. Some of them were fifteen years older than he was. He had only just stopped thinking of himself as a boy a few years before, and now he was expected to live among them as an equal, as an adult. *I didn't want to grow up so soon*, he thought. *But now I don't have any choice, I guess.*

The meal dragged on to its finish around 1330 hours. Commander Leswick appeared and announced a ninety-minute rest and recreation period. Boarding of the ship would commence at 1500 hours, sixty minutes before actual blastoff time.

They filed out of the mess hall – a hundred miscellaneous people, each carrying his own burden of fear and regret and resentment. Dawes walked along silently beside Phil Haas, the lawyer from Los Angeles. As they reached the door, Haas smiled and said, 'Did you leave a girl friend behind, Mike?'

Dawes was startled by the sudden intrusion on his reverie.

'Oh – ah – no, I guess not. There wasn't anybody special. I figured I couldn't afford to get very deeply involved, not with four years of medical school ahead of me. Not to mention interning and all the rest.'

'I know what you mean. I got married during my senior year at UCLA. We had a hard time of it while I was going to law school.'

'You – were married?'

Haas nodded. They stepped out into the open air. There was no lawn, just bare brown earth running to the borders of the starport. 'I have – had – two children,' he said. 'The boy's going to be seven, the girl five.'

'At least now your wife's not eligible for selection herself,' Dawes said.

'Only if she doesn't remarry. And I asked her to remarry, you see. She's not the sort of woman who can get along without a man around.' A momentary cloud passed over Haas' bony face. 'Another two years and I would have been safe. Well, that's the way it goes, I guess. Take it easy, Mike. I suppose I'll see you at 1500 hours.' Haas clapped Dawes genially on the shoulder and strode away.

Dawes felt his mood of depression beginning to lift. If a man like Haas could give up his home and his wife and his children at the age of thirty-eight, and still remain calm and able to smile, then it was wrong for anyone else to sulk. Sulking was useless, now. *But it's hard to talk yourself into being glad you were selected*, Dawes thought.

He thought a moment about Haas' wife. Haas' widow, for so she was legally, now; the wife of a selectee was legally widowed the moment his ship blasted off, and she was entitled to collect insurance, widow's pensions, and any other such benefits. But perhaps she didn't want to be a widow; perhaps she was willing and anxious to volunteer and go alongside her husband.

The law said no. She had to remain behind, willy-nilly, to rear her children. No wonder so many people remained childless these days. If you had children, you ran too many risks. A childless wife could always follow her husband to the stars, or vice versa. So, in a way, selection served as a population control, not only by removing people from Earth – a statistically insignificant six thousand a day – but by the much more efficient method of discouraging people from having children. In a world of seven billion people, anything that lessened population pressure was valuable. Even something as heartless as selection.

Dawes saw a bulletin board on the wall of the mess hall building. He wandered over. Tacked on it was a mimeographed roster of the *Gegenschein* passengers. Only four married couples were included in the hundred names. Dawes wondered how many of the other ninety-two had been married at the time of their selection. A good many, most likely. And how many husbands or wives had been unable to bring themselves to volunteer and thus join their selected mates? How many were leaving children behind?

How many, he wondered, welcomed selection as a chance to escape an intolerable marriage, an unpleasant job, a dreary and useless existence? Selection was not completely a curse, to some.

He returned to his room. The suitcase, he noticed, had been picked up while he had been gone. He sprawled out on the uncomfortable bed, kicked off his shoes, and waited for the time to pass.

At 1500 hours, the gong in the hall rang again. The crisp voice out of the speaker said, 'Attention. Attention. All selectees are to report to the front of the barracks for boarding ship, at once.'

In the hall, Dawes met Mary Elliot; the older woman smiled at him, and he returned the smile tensely. Several selectees whom Dawes did not know joined them at the elevator, and they rode down together.

'Well, this is it,' Mary Elliot said. 'Goodbye to Earth. I thought this week would never end!'

'So did I!' exclaimed a willowy thirtyish brunette behind Dawes. 'So long to Earth.'

Three motor coaches waited outside the barracks. Guards in blue-and-yellow uniforms efficiently herded the selectees into the first coach until it was full, then began channelling people toward the second. Dawes boarded the third coach. By that time, the first one was halfway across the immense spacefield. The uniformed men did their job with a calm impersonality that seemed faintly inhuman to Dawes. But, he reflected, they had to do this three times a week. All over the world, now, people were being herded into starships. By nightfall six thousand Earthmen would be on their way to an uncertain destination.

Close up, the *Gegenschein* seemed immense. Standing

81

upright on its tail, it reared two hundred feet above the scorched brown soil. Its hull was plated with a molecule-thick sheath of gold, by way of ornament; each of the starships had its own distinctive color. The hatch was sixty feet above the ground. To gain entry, one had to ride up a gantry lift that held five people at a time. A catwalk was available for those who wanted to climb.

Dawes was in no hurry. He waited in line for his turn to enter the lift. Turning, he took his last look at Earth, sucked in his last breath of Earth's air.

It was mid-afternoon. In the quiet isolation of the star-field the air had a clear, transparent quality. There was a tangy nip in it; it smelled of distant fir and spruce. The sun was low in the October sky, and a brisk breeze swept in from the north.

Now, at the moment of ship boarding, Dawes began to think of all he would never see again. Never another sunset on Earth, never the moon full and pale in the sky, never the familiar constellations. Never again the glory of autumn-tinted maples, never the sight of football players racing down a field, never again a hot dog or a hamburger or a vanilla sundae. Little things; but little things added up to a world, and it was a world he was leaving forever behind.

'Next five,' came the guard's voice.

Dawes shuffled forward and onto the metal platform. The lift rose with a groaning of winches. Now that he was close to the ship's skin, he could see the tiny pittings and indentations that told of previous service. The *Gegenschein* looked newly minted at a distance, but at close range the appearance was far different.

The lift halted at the lip of the entry hatch. Hands gathered them in, and behind Dawes the lift began to descend for its next load. Within, fluorescent lights cast their cold beams on a circular room which opened onto a spiral companionway at either end.

'Men go up, women down,' chanted a space-tanned young man in starman's uniform. 'Men to the fore compartment, women aft.'

Dawes clambered up the ladder that lined the companionway at the top of the circular room. He realized that, in flight, gyroscopic balancers would keep the ship forever upright – but it was difficult to visualize the way the compartments would be oriented.

At the top of the ladder another crewman waited. 'Men's dorm is straight ahead,' he was told.

Dawes found himself in a compartment large enough for twenty-five persons. There was nothing luxurious about the compartment: no money had been expended on plush carpeting, mosaic tile walls, or the other trimmings customary in commercial spacecraft. The walls were bare metal, unpainted, unornamented.

Dawes recognized Sid Nolan, the engineer from Tulsa, already sprawled out in one of the acceleration cradles. Dawes nodded hello and said, 'What are we supposed to do, now that we're here?'

'Just pick out a cradle and sit down. Once everybody's aboard they'll tell us what happens next.'

'Mind if I take this one?' Dawes asked, indicating the cradle that adjoined Nolan's.

'Why should I mind? Suit yourself.'

Dawes lowered himself into the cradle. It was like an oversize lounge chair, suspended on shockproof cables. At right and left there dangled safety straps to be buckled before blastoff.

The chamber filled quickly. Dawes recognized Ky Noonan, the husky volunteer, who entered, picked out a cradle, and immediately strapped himself in with an expert hand. Ed Sanderson, the accountant from Milwaukee, was three cradles to Dawes' left.

Dawes' watch said 1520 hours when the chamber was filled. A loudspeaker overhead crackled into life.

'Settlers of the planet Osiris, welcome aboard the starship *Gegenschein*,' a deep, pleasantly resonant voice said. 'I'm Captain McKenzie, and for the next four weeks I'll be in command of your ship. The compartments you now are in will be your residences for the entire journey – but you won't be as cooped up as it may seem now. There are two lounges, one fore and one aft, and a galley where you'll take your meals.

'The *Gegenschein* carries a crew of nine, and you'll meet them all soon enough. But I'll have to point out now that this isn't exactly a luxury liner. My crewmen have their own jobs to do, such as navigating, controlling the fuel flow, servicing the ship in flight. You'll be responsible for the tidiness of your own cabins, and each day ten of you will serve with the crew to help prepare meals and clean the ship.

'Blastoff will take place, as you know, at 1600 hours. The time is now 1523 hours, so, as you see, there are approximately thirty-seven minutes left. The countdown is in its final stages now. At 1545 hours you will all have to be strapped into your cradles; those of you who have travelled in space before may be familiar with the way the straps work, but in any event crewmen will circulate among you to make sure you're all strapped down.

'The ship will rise on conventional chemical-fuel rockets, as in interplanetary traffic. The initial acceleration will be three gravities; you may experience some discomfort, but not for long.

'We will travel on rocket drive for eighty-three minutes. At 1723 hours the rocket drive will cease to be operative, and we will make the Einsteinian conversion to nospace at 1730 hours. Once the conversion is complete you will be free to leave your protective cradles. There'll

84

be a signal given to indicate this. At 1800 hours dinner will be served in the galley.

'We'll continue on Einstein Drive for the next four weeks. In case any of you intend to get a last look at Earth as we blast off, please be informed now that there are no vision outlets or pickups anywhere in the ship but in the main control cabin. The reason for this is simple: any kind of porthole constitutes a structural weakness in the hull, and since better than 99% of the trip is going to be spent in nospace, where there's nothing to see anyway, the designing engineers have eliminated the visual outlets.

'Let me ask you now simply to relax, lie back, and get to know your neighbour. Blastoff time is thirty-five minutes from now. Thank you.'

The speaker clicked off.

Nolan murmured, 'Too bad about that business of no vision outlets. I would have liked to get a last look at the Earth on the way out.'

'Maybe it's better this way,' Dawes said.

'Yeah,' Nolan agreed after a pause. 'You may be right there.'

They fell silent. Dawes fumbled with the straps of his protective cradle; they locked into each other in an intricate way, but he solved it after a few moments of tentative fumbling, and by the time the crewman entered the compartment to check, Dawes was completely strapped down.

Minutes ticked away. Dawes tried to freeze in his mind the image of the moon full in the night sky, the Big Dipper, the belt of Orion. Less than ten minutes remained now.

He tried to picture the layout of the ship. At the very top, at the rounded nose, the control cabin and crew quarters were probably located. Then, he thought, below that were the two male dormitories, one on each side of the ship. Then the central lounge, and below that the two female dorms. In the rear, the other lounge, and the galley. And behind them, the rocket combustion chambers and the mysterious compartment housing the Einstein Drive.

He knew very little about the Einstein Drive. Only that its core was a thermonuclear generator that, by establishing a controlled field of greater than solar intensity, creased a stress-pattern in the fabric of space. And that the ship would nose through the stress-pattern like a seal gliding through a cleft in the Arctic ice, and the ship would enter the realm termed nospace.

And then? Somehow, travelling faster than the normal universe's limiting velocity, that of light, the *Gegenschein* would breast the gulf of light-years and emerge from nospace in the vicinity of Vega, to make a landing on Osiris by conventional chemical-rocket propulsion.

He frowned. He understood the principles only vaguely; hardly anyone really knew what happened when the Einstein generator went into action. All that counted was the result: and it worked. Without the development of the drive, in the late years of the twenty-first century, there would have been no expansion into the universe by Earthmen, no colony worlds, no selection. Perhaps a ship or two might have been despatched to Alpha Centauri, taking twelve years for the journey and return, or perhaps an immense vessel would have been sent starward to house several generations on a century-long flight to the stars.

Now, ships flitted from Earth to Vega in four weeks. And Terran colonies dotted the skies.

Dawes forced himself to relax. Somewhere above him, he knew, the countdown was in its final minutes. The field was clear; soon, with a mighty splash of radiance against the already seared soil, the *Gegenschein* would rear skyward.

'Stand by for blastoff,' the voice of Captain McKenzie warned suddenly.

Far beneath him, Dawes sensed the rumbling of the giant rocket engines. There was a thunderous roar; a massive fist pushed down, against his chest, as the ship lifted. His heart pounded furiously under the strain of acceleration. He closed his eyes.

He felt the pang of separation. His last bond with Earth, the bond of gravity, had been severed.

CHAPTER NINE

Dawes had never known four weeks could move so slowly.

The novelty of being spaceborne wore off almost at the beginning. In nospace, there was no sense of motion, no rocket vibration, no feeling of acceleration. The ship hung motionless. And the hundred passengers, crammed mercilessly into their tiny vessel, began to feel like prisoners in a large cell.

During that first week, the hundred colonists concentrated on getting to know each other – but in a distant, guarded way, as if each had something to hide from all the others, that something being his inmost self. After a week, Dawes knew the names of almost all of his fellow selectees, but he knew little else about them. Each of the hundred cloaked himself in his private tragedy and made little effort to form friendships.

There were exceptions. Phil Haas, the West Coast lawyer who had left wife and children behind, circulated among the entire group, making friends, talking to people, encouraging them, soothing them. Mary Elliot, the plump, motherly woman who was the oldest of all the hundred selectees at thirty-nine, did the same. And soon it became evident that Haas would be an ideal Colony Director, with Mary Elliot as his wife.

The ship was cramped. There was hardly any room in the sleeping quarters except for sleeping; the lounges aft were small and low of ceiling, while the galley just barely held all of them at table. The narrow companionways that ran the length of the ship would pass two abreast, no more. There was little in the way of recreation aboard ship: a few books, a few music-tapes, nightly film showings. Most of the books and music and films were stowed away in the cargo hold with the other possessions of the colony-to-be.

As 'day' dragged into 'day' and week into week, Dawes found himself going stale with the monotony and constant discomfort. He counted days, then hours, until landing. He slept as much as he could, sometimes fifteen and sixteen hours a day, until he could sleep no more.

Little cliques were forming aboard the ship as the weeks passed. Groups of six or eight took shape: people from the same geographical area, or people of the same general age and intelligence groups, who saw something to share in their common misfortune. Dawes joined none of these groups. He was the youngest member of the colony, at twenty – by some fluke of the computer, none of the other men was less than twenty-five, and most were in their early thirties – and he stood to one side, unable to mingle at ease with the older people. Many of them had lost wives, families, homes that had been built and furnished with care and expense, jobs that had cost them outlay of energy and vigorous exertion. He felt guilty, in a way, that he had lost nothing more serious than his education and his chosen profession. Conscious that the other selectees were adults and he himself something less than that, though more than a boy, Dawes established and observed the gulf between them, and made few friends.

In the third week an election was held. Phil Haas was chosen Colony Director, running unopposed. He announced that he would serve for one year and then would hold new elections. The colonists assembled, granted him the right to rule by decree until a constitution could be adopted, and some sort of colonial council established.

Dawes wondered about the unanimity of the election. Certainly their were other men among the fifty who yearned for power. Why had they kept politely silent while Haas was being acclaimed? Men like Dave Matthews, Lee Donaldson: strong men, capable men, outspoken men. Perhaps they were just biding their time, Dawes thought. Waiting, letting Haas handle the difficult task of getting the colony in motion, then making their bids.

Dawes shrugged. *He* had no interest in playing politics. He kept to himself, intending to do his job as a colonist as best he could, without looking for trouble. Let others fight among themselves for responsibilities; he was content to drift passively along. After all, he thought, he hadn't asked to be sent here. Nor was he going to ask for any great share in the responsibilities.

At the end of the fourth week, finally – it seemed like the fourth century since blasting off from Earth – a ship-wide announcement sent the Osiris colonists scuttling back to their protective cradles.

'The time is 1443 hours, ship time. In exactly twelve minutes, at 1455 hours, we're going to make a transition out of nospace and back to rocket drive. We'll enter the atmosphere of Osiris at 1600 hours and take three hours to complete our landing orbit. We'll touch down on the day-side of Osiris at 1900 hours, which will be exactly noonday down below. Everybody strap down now.'

Dawes' fingers quivered nervously as he lashed himself into the acceleration cradle. This was it! Landing in less than five hours!

He wondered about Osiris. The Colonization Bureau had prepared a couple of mimeographed sheets about the planet for distribution to the colonists, but the information on them was scanty. He knew that the planet was roughly Earthsize – 8100 miles in diameter – and that the soil was arable; that the air was like the air of Earth, only with a trifle less oxygen, a trifle more nitrogen, not enough of a difference to matter; that the planet had seven continents, of which two were polar and thus uninhabitable. Survey team reports were never tremendously reliable: the survey teams moved with desperate haste, often scouting an entire solar system in a day or two, and once they found a world to be reasonably suitable they rarely bothered to look for drawbacks. According to the survey team report, there was no intelligent life on Osiris, at least not on the temperate northern continent that had been chosen for the colony. It was an easy statement to make; so far intelligent life had been discovered nowhere else in the universe. Many planets had species no more than a hundred thousand years away from intelligence, but nowhere but on Earth was there a culture, a civilization, as much as a language. Or so the findings had been so far.

At 1455 hours came the shock of transition. The Einstein generator lashed out, smashing a gap in the fabric of nospace, and the *Gegenschein* slipped through the aperture and back into the universe of real things. Instantly the rocket engines came into play, guiding the ship into orbit round the planet below. In a series of ever-narrowing spirals the *Gegenschein* would glide downward, matching velocities with Osiris, until its path grazed the skin of the planet and the ship came to rest at last.

Lying pinioned in his acceleration cradle, Mike Dawes clenched his teeth against the pounding of the rockets. The *Gegenschein* was not insulated very well against engine vibration; it was strictly functional, a tube designed to transport people from one world to another, without pretensions to comfort.

He regretted the lack of a vision screen. It might have been inspiring to see Osiris growing steadily ahead as the *Gegenschein* landed. Much more inspiring than lying on your back in a badly ventilated compartment, Dawes thought, lying in the half-darkness. Somewhere ahead in the night was Osiris, Vega IX, four billion miles from the fourth brightest star in Earth's sky. Would Sol be visible in Osiris' night sky? Probably – as an insignificant white dot of negligible magnitude.

No one spoke as the *Gegenschein* plunged planetward. Each man in the compartment was alone with his dreams and memories now. The minutes passed; at 1600 hours Captain McKenzie announced that the ship had entered Osiris' atmosphere at last. The actual landing was still three hours away, as the ship swung round the planet, coming closer and closer to the surface.

1900 hours. Within his cradle Mike Dawes struggled to keep his stomach under control. The last hour had been a bumpy, bouncing ride downward through thickening layers of atmosphere. Atmospheric eddies jounced the golden ship; a storm layer buffeted it. But the journey was ending. The *Gegenschein* hung low over Osiris' northern temperate continent, dropping, dropping . . .

Landing.

The impact shuddered through the ship. The *Gegenschein* wobbled only an instant before the landing-jacks took effect, digging into the ground.

Captain McKenzie said, 'We've landed right on the nose. Welcome to Osiris, ladies and gentlemen.'

We're here, Dawes thought.

He longed to burrow through the ship's wall and see the new planet. But an hour more passed before the colonists could leave the ship. First, the routine atmospheric tests ('as if they'll take us all back home if they discover that the air's pure helium,' Sid Nolan grumbled.)

Then, the cooling-off period of fifteen minutes while nozzles beneath the ship's belly sluiced decontaminating fluids onto the landing area to deal with the radiation products and chemical poisons of the rocket exhaust.

After that, the opening of the hatch, the lowering of the catwalk. No gantry lift waiting for them; descent from the ship would be by ladder only. Phil Haas and Mary Elliot were the first people out; after them came the others, filing in slow shuffle along the companionway until they reached the hatch.

Dawes was the twentieth to leave the ship. He stepped out onto the lip of the hatch.

Osiris lay before him. The ship had landed in a clearing at the shore of a glittering blue lake. Beyond the expanse of pinkish-red sand, the soil became more fertile; not far away loomed a dark, ominous-looking forest, and high beyond rose arching black cliffs.

Gray clouds lay heavily in the dark-blue sky like greasy puffs of wool. High overhead burned giant Vega, with its disc the apparent size of the sun of Earth, even at a distance of four billion miles. The air smelled subtly different – thin, with a salt tang to it that was nothing like the tang of the open ocean. And it was cold. The temperature was about fifty, but an icy wind came sleeting down out of the forest, cutting into him as he stood staring sixty feet above the ground.

He hadn't expected it to be this cold. For no specific reason he had anticipated tropic heat. But Osiris, at least this continent at this time of year, seemed bleak, inhospitable, uninviting.

'Come on, kid,' someone said behind him. 'Don't stand there all day. Get down the ladder.'

Dawes smiled apologetically. 'Sorry. Just taking it all in.'

'You've got plenty of time for that.'

Dawes reddened and scrambled hastily down the cat-walk. The others were waiting below. The pinkish sand crunched underfoot. Feeling for the first time, Dawes thought with awe and wonder, the touch of a human foot.

Chill winds swept down on him as he stood huddling into himself for warmth, waiting for Haas to organize things, to take charge. As the colonists filed out of the ship, they wandered about aimlessly on the sand, moving without direction or purpose or words, all of them struggling to minimize the shock of concrete realization that they were alone on an alien planet, never to see Earth again.

At last all hundred had disembarked, as well as Captain McKenzie and his crew.

Haas had obtained a whistle from somewhere. He blew it now.

'Attention! Attention, everybody!'

The wanderers returned to the group. Silence fell. The wind hooted through the distant forest.

Haas said, 'Captain McKenzie tells me that he intends to blast off for Earth as soon as possible. Our first job, then, is to unload the ship. We'll do it in bucket-brigade fashion. Noonan, pick a team of five men and go with Captain McKenzie: you'll be the ones to get the crates out of the ship. Sanderson, choose three and arrange yourselves near the ship to take the crates as they come out. We'll pass them along until they've been placed over there, at the end of the beach, beyond the five hundred yard safety zone the *Gegenschein* is going to need.' Haas paused. 'Matthews, take four colonists and go scouting around the area. Look around for any lurking wildlife, and yell if you see anything. The rest of you just stay in the area; no wandering off.'

Dawes was passed over by the heads of the teams; he

shrugged, thrust his hands in his pockets, and stood to one side. The cargo hatch in the belly of the ship was lowered open, and Noonan and his team entered, while the *Gegenschein* crew clambered back up the catwalk to ready their ship for departure. In a few minutes, crates began appearing, heavy wire-bound wooden crates that contained all of Earth that there had been room to bring along.

Others lugged the crates across the clearing, out of the way of the ship's rocket-blast area. The job took nearly an hour. Haas inventoried each crate as it appeared, checking it off against a master list. When half had appeared, he whistled again and rotated the teams, letting the tired men rest and putting fresh ones to work. Dawes took his place in the second team, hauling the crates away from the ship and over to the supply dump.

The cargo hold was nearly empty when Dave Matthews came trotting out of the forest, shouting for Haas.

The colony director turned. 'What is it, Dave?'

Matthews raced up, panting. Dawes and a few others stopped work to listen to him.

Matthews gasped, 'Aliens! I saw aliens!'

Haas frowned. 'What?'

'Skulking around in the edge of the forest. Dark shadowy things. They looked like men, or apes, or something.'

A twinge of fear went through Dawes. But Haas smiled. 'Are you sure, Dave?'

'How can I be sure? They ran away as soon as I went toward them.'

'Did anyone else in your team see them?' Haas asked, looking at the other four members of the scouting patrol.

'Not me,' Sid Nolan said.

'Me neither,' Paul Wilson agreed. 'We came running when Matthews shouted, but we didn't see anything.'

'And the survey team said there was no intelligent life on Osiris,' Nolan pointed out.

Haas shrugged the matter off. 'We'll check later. You might have been mistaken, Dave.'

'I hope so. But I wasn't.'

The affair was allowed to drop there. At the moment, it was more urgent to empty out the *Gegenschein*.

The work made Dawes perspire, and then he felt colder when a gust of wind came. But he enjoyed the mere activity of moving around, of using his muscles after four weeks of dreary confinement.

At last the ship was unloaded. An assortment of packing-crates and smaller cases sat in disorder five hundred yards from the ship. The crewman bustled busily about, checking off items on a vastly accelerated count-down. It took two days to prepare a ship for blastoff when it was laden with colonists and cargo; empty, it could be readied in only a few hours.

While the crewman worked, the hundred colonists boarded the ship for the last time, to prepare a meal in the galley. It would be their third meal of the day. But it was only midday on Osiris, and Haas had ordered that work would continue until sundown, six or seven hours hence, so they would be adjusted to the new time-schedule from the very start. Dawes was on the clean-up crew after the meal. When he emerged from the ship, finally, he saw Haas and Captain McKenzie in conference. Haas was counting, to make certain everyone was off the ship.

He blew his whistle. 'Attention, all! The *Gegenschein* is about to blast off! Everyone over by the cargo, right away! The *Gegenschein* is leaving!'

CHAPTER TEN

Final preparations took twenty minutes. At last, the *Gegenschein* was ready. It sounded one last warning honk before blasting off. Mike Dawes, standing in the safe zone with the other colonists, felt a sharp inward tug as he saw the ship seem to draw back on its haunches, retracting its landing jacks in the last few moments before blastoff. This was the last link with Earth, the golden ship at the edge of the lake.

The warning honk died away and the ship sprang suddenly up from the ground, hovering on its blazing pillar of flame for a moment as it fought with Osiris' pull, then, breaking loose, shot upward to the cloud-muddied sky. For half a minute, perhaps, the retreating rocket-blast added a second sun to the sky. A strange luminous glow cast double shadows over the ground, but faded rapidly. The *Gegenschein* was gone.

A life hardly begun was finished now, Dawes realized. His past, twenty years on Earth, infancy and childhood and awkward adolescence, was becoming remote and dreamlike, as if it had not actually happened to him but had been told to him in sleep. Only the uncertain future was real.

He stood by himself, nervously staring at the seared place where the *Gegenschein* had been. Beyond lay the dark forest, either inhabited or not inhabited by humanoid alien beings, depending on the accuracy of Dave

Matthews' observation. Dawes felt cold. This was not a pleasant world.

And blastoff had been like the severing of the umbilicus. A thunder of flame and a bull-voiced roar and the link with Mother Earth was severed forever.

Severing of the umbilicus. He liked the analogy. It was the sort of thought a doctor might have. And he was a doctor in embryo only, or not even that – a shivering skinny twenty-year-old who would never have to worry about medical school applications now. A flip of the wheel, a random twitch of the giant computer, and they packed you off like a steer on a tenth-class ship to a world like Osiris. They ripped you out of your old life and told you to build a new one, on a cold windswept planet where shadowy alien shapes skulked through the dismal forest.

A hand grabbed Dawes' shoulder firmly from behind, breaking into his mood. He looked around.

'Something the matter with you?' Ky Noonan asked gruffly. 'You look lousy.'

'I feel lousy. Mind?'

Noonan grinned. 'It's your privilege, kid. But you better stop brooding about Earth.'

'I'm not—'

'I see it all over your face. Look, Earth don't exist any more, as far as you and me are concerned. There's just Osiris.'

'I know that,' Dawes said slowly. 'But it takes a while to get used to the idea.'

'You've had plenty of time. Four weeks on the ship, and two hours since we landed. Take some free advice: get used to being here.'

Dawes made no reply. All the time since the day he had pulled the blue envelope from his mailbox, he had been telling himself to accept the dealings of fate without complaint. He had deluded himself into thinking he was resigned to selection. But evidently he wasn't. Apparently the resentment still showed in his eyes.

Noonan chuckled and strode lightly away, toward a small group of women on the other side of the packing cases. Dawes followed him with his eyes, brow furrowing as he strained to understand what made the big man tick.

Noonan was a volunteer. He wore his volunteer's status like a badge of merit, which it was. Dawes watched him bantering with the girls over there. The big man was smiling, but there was a faraway look in his eyes. Still, he seemed completely at ease, self-sufficient, happy. As if anyone could be happy, torn from family, friends, career—

No. Dawes reminded himself that Noonan had *volunteered*. He hadn't been torn from anything; maybe he had nothing to be torn from.

Phil Haas mounted a packing crate at the far end of the clearing and blew his whistle. It was time to get things set up. Dawes joined the gathering group.

'We're on our own now,' Haas said, speaking loudly to fight the insistent whistling of the wind. 'That ship is gone and it isn't ever coming back. We've got plenty to do now. The first thing is to set up the stockade and inflate the domes.'

A voice from the back of the group – Dave Matthews' voice – called out. 'Phil, what about those aliens I saw? I think we ought to have a permanent security patrol, just in case they come back.'

Haas' lean face darkened. 'The important thing is to get the stockade built immediately.'

'But the aliens—'

'There's some doubt as to whether you actually did see aliens, Dave. Remember, the survey team didn't find any such creatures here—'

'How long did they look? Half an hour?'

Haas said with a trace of impatience, 'Dave, if you want to discuss this further, take it up in private with me. We can't spare men for a patrol until the stockade's been built. Besides which, your aliens, if they exist, are probably more afraid of us than we are of them.' Haas chuckled. 'Let's get busy. We've got plenty more things to do by nightfall – including the marrying.'

Dawes moistened his lips. Yes, the marrying! He had pushed the thought into the back of his mind, but now there was no avoiding it.

He drew his jacket tighter around himself. Like most thin people, he had little use for cold weather; the wind seemed to cut right through his jacket and between his ribs. The survey team report had said Osiris was Earth-type, uninhabited, and fairly fertile, but they hadn't said anything about that damned nor-wester that ripped down constantly from the forest.

Haas stepped down from his packing crate and called over Noonan, Stoker, Donaldson, and several of the other stronger men of the group, to discuss plans for setting up the colony. According to the booklets that had been distributed before landing, there was a fixed and time-tested procedure for setting up a new colony – a procedure that had worked well on the hundreds of worlds to which humanity had already spread.

The first step was to establish a stockade, to mark the original boundaries of the colony and to provide a tangible measure of the colony's foothold, as well as to serve in keeping stray alien creatures away.

Once the stockade was up, the bubble-houses went up, the homes of the colonists. No more the painstaking hewing of logs for cabins; the bubble-houses sprouted simply and easily from the extrusion nozzles. A gallon of the self-polymerizing fluid could serve to create homes for thousands of colonists; once it was gone, the science of architecture would begin on the new world.

Once the fifty couples were settled, the next matter was that of being fruitful and multiplying. Since the colonists were screened for fertility, it was reasonable to expect thirty or forty offspring in the first year of the colony, twenty or thirty in each succeeding year. By the time ten years had passed, the older children would be able to care for the new crop of babies. After fifteen years, the total population of the colony might be as much as five hundred – and the first second-generation marriages would be taking place. Given unlimited space and no economic problems, breeding could be unlimited for several generations. Population would expand: eight hundred, a thousand, fifteen hundred. It leaped upward by exponential bounds in each generation. And the colony spread outward into the alien wilds, until the raw settlement became a village, a city, a city among other cities. One by one, a series of new Earths would thus be carved across the reaches of space by grumbling, miserable, conscripted pioneers.

Haas took a while to formulate his plans for the first day's work. Dawes waited at the edge of the clearing. The idle colonists, in no hurry to receive their orders, had formed into the shipboard cliques again. Eight or nine women stood in one bleakfaced little clump not far away, their faces reflecting their realization of where they were and how dead their past lives were. Further away Dawes saw a circle composed of the younger unmarried men, joking tensely, nudging each other in the ribs. The four married couples – The Wilsons, Zacharies, Frys and Nortons – remained apart, as if emphasizing the fact that they would not be concerned with the mass mating soon to take place.

Dawes stole a look at the little group of women. At least

half of them were far too old for him to begin to consider as potential mates. If he had last choice, he might indeed have one of them thrust at him, but he hoped not.

Most of the women were in their middle or late twenties. Carol Herrick, at twenty-two, was closest to his own age. Dawes looked at her. She was shivering slightly in the cold wind, tugging her lightweight jacket closed. She was a slim girl with brown hair, black eyes, and a kind of dewy-faced prettiness about her. Dawes had not exchanged many words with her in the four weeks, only the standard introductions. She seemed shy, as shy as he, and he liked that. She was bound to catch the eye of one of the older men, and whoever preceded him in the picking would probably grab her up.

He wondered about the other girls. Cherry Thomas, for instance; he heard her loud laughter as she stood joking with some of the men. She was tall, lively, sophisticated-looking. She looked to be about twenty-five or so, and she looked as if she'd been around a lot in her time. The impartial scoop of the lottery seized all kinds.

What of the others? Claire Lubetkin, she of the nervous tic and the faint predisposition toward hysteria? Chunky, dark-haired Louise Marino, who seemed to have spent a man-starved life? Some of the women had never been married; others had husbands, now widowers, on Earth, against whom they were bound to measure any new mate.

A strange uneasiness stole over Dawes and he turned his attention away from the women. One of them would be his wife, on this bitter, wind-tossed world. He would know which one soon enough.

Haas had finished working out his plans. He whistled once again for attention.

'The order of business right now is to get the stockade up. You've been divided into six work gangs. Gangs one, two, and three will be led by Ky Noonan, Howard Stoker and myself. We'll distribute blasters to those three gangs and you'll gather tree-trunks for the backbone of the stockade. Work gang four will be under Sid Nolan, and that gang will be in charge of placing the trunks in the ground. Work gang five, under Lee Donaldson, will bind the trunks together with permospray. Work gang six, under Mary Elliot, will unpack the crates and provisions.'

It was neatly arranged. Most of the men were assigned to the three logging groups. Dawes and sixteen others went into Nolan's group, which did the actual building of the stockade. The women were split between Donaldson's group and Mary Elliot's.

The work went smoothly enough, thanks to the tools supplied by Earth. The forest was thick with barkless trees twenty feet high and six or eight inches in diameter; the three logging groups made swift work of burning them down, trimming away the limbs and the fragrant needley foliage, and sizing the trees to a uniform twenty-foot length. It took only a few minutes to prepare each tree; within half an hour, several dozen were stacked at the border between the forest and the clearing.

At that point, Nolan's group went into action. They had already laid out their boundaries, and now it was a simple matter of scooping out a pit with the vacuum extractor, shoving the sharpened point of the trunk some four feet into the ground, and tamping down the ground. Dawes hove to with the rest, feeling a pleasant thrill at the thought that the colony was under way, that his hands were helping to shape its walls.

As the row of stakes grew, placed regularly in the ground three feet apart, Donaldson followed along with the extrusion machine, spewing out a binding layer of plastic between each wooden rib. And within the stockade boundaries the women worked, ripping into the sealed crates and laying bare their contents.

After nearly two hours of steady work, the stockade had taken definite shape on three sides. After three hours, it was practically finished, and Haas and his crew, no longer required to supply more logs, were fashioning the gate and bolt for the stockade's entrance. Already the place seemed snug, the winds less cruel, Dawes thought. He felt exhausted from his work, the constant hoisting of logs and placing them in the ground, but it was a good kind of exhaustion, the warm feeling of constructive exertion.

Nightfall came. Giant Vega had dipped far below the horizon, and a sprinkling of unfamiliar constellations brightened the darkening sky. No moon had risen. But, by floodlights, the work had gone on. The stockade was nearly perfect, having sprung up miraculously in only a few hours. And the bubble-houses had been blown: fifty of them, small opaque blue domes that glinted dully in the floodlights' glare. A fifty-first dome, larger than the rest, stood in the very center of the stockade. It would be the central gathering-place of the colony in the early days.

Dawes hunkered down on his heels, resting. He was tired; his muscles would ache in the morning. But the colony was off to a flying start. The stockade was built and the homes were erected.

'Swell job, everyone,' Haas congratulated them. 'We're right on schedule. And it's wonderful the way you all pitched in and did your share.'

'What about wives?' Noonan asked loudly.

A tense, apprehensive giggle began among the women, and rapidly spread through the group. Haas held up his hand for silence. 'I was just getting to that part of it now. It's the one remaining item of business.'

The women looked strained, oddly tense, as Haas organized them into a group for the mate-picking. Dawes studied their faces. Cherry Thomas was smiling. Some of the other women looked worried, pale, tense. Those were the ones who had never been married, who had dreamed of a different sort of wedding night, before their number came up. Others, those who had left husbands behind on Earth, were obviously thinking of their loved ones trillions of miles away.

Haas unfolded a sheet of paper and frowned. 'The time has come to couple off. The instructions I have suggest the following recommended procedure for handling this: as a volunteer, Ky Noonan has the right to take first pick. As colony director, I get second pick. After that, we proceed in order of computer registration number – an order known only to me, at the moment. I think that way is better than any other system, and unless I hear any strong objections that'll be the method we'll use.'

No one spoke. Dawes privately wished that someone would speak up in favor of a more gradual system – say, letting things take their natural course, couples forming as the days went by. But colonies were warned against such arrangements. It was far safer to establish couplings right at the start, having everyone in the small community settled at once.

'Very well,' Haas said. 'We'll go down the list. Each man will select a woman, but she has the right of refusal. In case your choice refuses you, you don't get to pick again until every other man has spoken. If anyone remains uncoupled after three run-throughs, I'll make assignments myself. Okay. Noonan, as a volunteer you've earned the privilege of picking first. Step forward and name your choice.'

Noonan came forward, smiling calmly. He was the biggest, most aggressive male in the group, and he gloried in the confident knowledge of his own superiority.

He ran his eyes insouciantly down the row of waiting

women. A strange mixture of emotions appeared on fifty feminine faces. Some of the women seemed fearful of being picked by him, others openly hostile, others pleadingly anxious.

After a moment of hushed silence, Noonan said, 'All right. I pick Cherry Thomas.'

Dawes let his breath out explosively. He had been certain that Noonan would pick Carol Herrick – but he had bypassed her in favor of the older woman, for some reason.

Haas said, 'Miss Thomas, is this choice agreeable?'

Cherry Thomas stared levelly at Noonan, appraising him frankly. 'I guess so,' she said. 'If Noonan wants me, I'll go with him.'

People snickered. A little testily, Haas said, 'This is marriage, Miss Thomas.'

'Don't hand me any damned piousness!' Cherry snapped. 'You aren't any better than me, and don't forget it! I—' she stopped. 'Okay. Sorry. Maybe I earned that crack. Okay, Noonan will do.'

Haas made an entry on his list. 'So be it. You can have your pick of any of the bubble-houses. Suppose I say now that any marriage can be dissolved on Osiris by approval of the council, once we have a council. Until then let's try not to have any split-ups.'

Dawes watched Noonan and Cherry stroll away to take their pick of house sites. *No ceremony?* He wondered. It didn't seem so. The simple act of picking solemnized the marriage. Well, Dawes thought, it's a brand-new world. Perhaps it's better this way.

Haas was next, and to no one's surprise picked Mary Elliot, who accepted. That was a foregone conclusion, of course.

The colony director looked down at his list again, and announced that Lee Donaldson had next pick. Donaldson, a strong, commanding-looking man, strode forward and announced his choice loudly: 'Clair Lubetkin.'

Claire reddened, fidgeted, nibbled her lower lip. Haas put the question to her. She wavered indecisively, glanced around at the other men, and finally nodded. 'I accept the choice.'

After Donaldson came Howard Stoker. He came forward in his bear-like, rumbling walk, with the dirt of his day's labor still clinging to him.

He eyed the women as if making up his mind at the last moment and said, 'Rina Morris.'

Ninety-odd pairs of eyes focused on Rina Morris. The redhaired girl drew herself up stiffly. She looked at the thickset, ugly Stoker with an expression that was anything but friendly. 'Sorry. I'll wait a turn.'

Stoker scowled at her angrily. 'Okay, If you're going to be that way, to hell with you. I pick Carol Herrick instead.

Dawes whitened at the thought of Stoker pawing over Carol. He wanted to shout out, to protest.

But Haas said, 'Sorry, Howard, I told you before that regulations don't give you a second choice until everyone else has spoken.'

'But—'

'You heard me, Stoker.'

'Dammit, I'm not going to wait at the end of the line! Just because that girl is too proud to have me, I—'

Haas said in a voice that suddenly crackled with authority, 'You'll do whatever I tell you to do, Howard. Get back in line and wait your turn. Mike Dawes has next choice.'

Stoker grumbled something, spat ostentatiously, and walked to the rear of the group. Dawes stumbled forth red-faced, still astonished at the sudden reprieve. Carol had been picked by Stoker, and Haas had refused to allow the choice, and now it was *his* choice—

A row of faces confronted him. Kindly maternal faces; frightened faces; amused faces. And one face above all others. Dawes searched for the words.

'I p-pick – I pick Carol Herrick.'

Haas smiled. 'Miss Herrick?'

Dawes waited for an agonizing span of time. He could not look at Carol's face. He stared away, at the ground, too tense to draw a breath.

Finally she said, in a voice so soft it could barely be heard, 'I accept.'

CHAPTER ELEVEN

Dawes and Carol left the clearing together, walking rapidly away without speaking, virtually without looking at each other.

He said to her finally, as they approached the circular row of bubble-houses, 'We'd better pick one out.'

'Pick any one you like – Mike.'

He glanced at them. The domes were empty, merely arching shelters against the downslanting winds, but they did provide a place to sleep if you didn't mind the ground. Colonists weren't supposed to mind little things like having to sleep on the ground until there was time to build beds.

He pointed at the bubble-house that adjoined Noonan's. It might be a good idea to have Noonan as a neighbor, Dawes thought. Just in case of trouble.

'Let's take that one,' Dawes said.

They walked toward it, Dawes carrying his own suitcase and hers, each with its twenty pounds of personal possessions. At the entrance to the dome he paused, wondering vaguely whether he should bother with the old ritual of carrying his wife across the threshold. He nearly put down the suitcases to turn to her; then, changing his mind, he simply walked inside the dome. She followed him in.

Within, the dome covered an area of perhaps two hundred square feet. There would be room for a bed and perhaps a clothes cabinet of some sort, not much else.

Plumbing would come a while later; until that time, they would have to make do with the nearby lake for washing and drinking.

'It isn't very impressive, is it?' he asked.

'No. Not very.'

'We'll fix it up. These domes are just temporary, just places to stay until we can begin building homes. We'll have a swell place some day, Carol.'

He smiled encouragingly at her. But she could not keep up the pretense; she sank down onto her suitcase and stared bleakly off into nowhere. Dawes began to wonder about the sleeping arrangements for the night. They would have to spread out all their clothes, he thought, and huddle together for warmth—

'I hadn't expected it to be like this,' she said suddenly in a toneless voice. 'I mean, my life, and all. I never really thought much about what I was going to do with myself. But I didn't figure I'd end up in a little bubble on some other world.'

'Neither did I. Neither did any of us, Carol.'

'But we're here, aren't we?'

He nodded, After a moment, he said, 'What did you do, on Earth?'

'Do? Oh – I was a stenographer, Typist, mostly. For a construction firm in Oakland. I guess I was just waiting around to get married, when the time came. Well, I guess the time *did* come – sort of.'

Dawes was disappointed. He had never asked her before – he had never dared to speak much with her on the ship – but he had privately hoped she had been an actress, a writer, perhaps a singer. Someone with a talent, someone he could be proud of, someone who would stand out from all the other women. He decided he would have to be content with her slim prettiness, and let all else go. She was, it seemed, just an ordinary girl, shyly innocent.

'I was going to college,' he said. 'Pre-med. Ohio State. Well, *that's* all finished, too. We have to start all over, here on Osiris.'

He laughed – a nervous, brittle laugh. The door of the bubble-house was still open; he shut it, looking outside first. The last rays of Vega had long since faded from the sky. Night had come. Dawes admitted to himself that he felt afraid of what night would bring. Alone in this chilly plastic bubble with this frightened girl, free in the eyes of the universe to do anything with her he cared to, if she would let him—

The conversation refused to become self-sustaining. It kept running out of fuel; three or four times Dawes forced himself to start a new topic, but after ten minutes he let the interchange sputter to a total halt. They were silent a while, watching each other.

'It's like a blind date,' Carol said quietly, when a few moments had passed. 'You and me, put together like this. A blind date that's for keeps.'

'Why did you say yes when I picked you?'

'What else could I do? I didn't want any of the others, the older men. You looked like somebody I could talk to, somebody I'd be happy with. Even if you are a little younger than me. It's better than going with one of those older ones.'

'I hope we're happy together, Carol.'

'I hope so, too. But – Mike, I'm afraid—'

There were tears in the edges of her eyes. Dawes realized that she was rapidly losing her nerve and might well go off into wild hysterics any moment. That wasn't the way he cared to spend his wedding night. And he wouldn't know how to handle her if she burst in tears.

He said as firmly as he could, 'We're going to have to make the most of things, Carol. You know what I mean. It's going to *be* this way, now that our number came up.

You and me, together on Osiris, and no turning back. Not ever.'

She nodded. And then, after a frozen moment of silence, he found himself moving toward her, putting his arms round her thin shoulders, kissing her. It was a tender, tremulous sort of kiss, a tentative contact of dry lips, and it had hardly begun when it was interrupted suddenly by a harsh yell coming from the general direction of Noonan's bubble at the left.

He pulled back from her. 'Did you hear something - a shout?'

'It sounded like it was Noonan. Do you think he's having trouble with Cherry?'

'I don't know. But—'

The shouts came again. And this time the words were unmistakable. Noonan was bellowing. *'Hey! Dawes! Dawes! Help!'*

'Let's see what's happening,' Dawes suggested.

He stepped outside the bubble, into solid moonless blackness. He blinked, trying to see.

After a moment his eyes adjusted to the darkness, and he saw what was taking place.

Noonan and Cherry were outside their dome. They were surrounded by dark shapes, black forms against the blackness. Noonan was flailing at the shapes and shouting.

'Get away from me!' the big man cried. 'Hey, Dawes! Run! Get help!'

Dawes froze, not knowing which way to turn. He heard Carol catch her breath sharply. His eyes, growing more accustomed to the dark, picked out the scene clearly now.

Six or seven dark stubby figures – unhuman figures – clustered around the struggling forms of Noonan and Cherry Thomas. Dawes saw hunched, neckless heads, thick shoulders, corded arms. He was too sick to run. He stood where he was, listening to Noonan's cursing, Cherry's fear-sharpened voice, and the occasional croaking grunt of a smitten attacker.

Then he felt something cold and hairy touch him, and he heard Carol scream.

Other colonists were coming. Dawes fought, fought for the first time since forgotten childhood. He fought with arms and legs, whirled and butted with his shoulders, kicked out at chunky, heavily furred figures he could only partially see. His nails clawed into a musky-smelling hide. He squirmed, wriggled, kicked again. And then he could fight no more. He was held tight, solidly clamped by thick alien arms.

'Mike!' Carol whimpered.

He felt a pang of inadequacy. 'I can't do anything, Carol. Not a thing. They've got me, too.'

'It's the aliens,' came Noonan's angry voice. 'The ones Matthews saw. Hostile aliens.' His booming cry seemed to carry all over the colony ground. 'Aliens!'

Dawes felt himself being hoisted from the ground. Two powerful hands gripped his ankles, two his shoulders. He tried once again to resist, but it was like trying to break loose from the grip of a hydraulic press.

He swayed. He realized he was moving.

Dark shapes, and darker jungle. He was being carried toward the forest. He could see nothing, neither Carol nor Noonan nor Cherry.

After a while, he stopped trying to break free. The aliens were handling him gently enough. He simply could not move, but they were carrying him along at a steady pace. Too bad there was no moon, he thought. He could make out the shadowy shapes of trees bending above him, but all else was indistinct. He heard night-birds crowing harshly, mocking him from the treetops. Fear enshrouded him; he was too frightened even to be afraid, any more. Carried along in the soft alien grip, he offered himself up to fate, knowing he had no alternative.

The journey went on for more than an hour. Perhaps it was two hours; it might just as well have been two months. Dawes lost all sense of the passage of time. The forest was surprisingly thick for such a cold continent. Dangling vines brushed his face, one of them leaving a nauseous trail of slime. His hands were in alien control; he could not even wipe his face. After a while the trail of slime, running down the left side of his face from eyebrow to the corner of his mouth, began to burn – whether for imaginary reasons or because of some chemically corrosive effect, Dawes could not tell. He twisted his head around and managed to rub some of the slime off on the shoulder of his shirt. But an inch or two remained, just to the left of his eye, tormenting him by its inaccessibility. He wondered if it would leave some sort of mark, perhaps a white scar or a puckering of the skin.

At last the trek through the forest came to its end. The aliens broke from the thicket and Dawes could see the bald, bare faces of jutting cliffs, the upthrust fangs of black rock that had looked so forbiddingly Gothic when he had first viewed them from the lip of the *Gegenschein*'s hatch.

He began to feel the ascent. Going up the side of the mountain was a terrifying experience – the most terrifying since the actual kidnapping.

The aliens, his night-sharpened eyes perceived, had thick bluish pads on their palms and on the soles of their blunt feet. Suction pads.

The aliens gripped him firmly, at shoulders and feet, and started to ascend the naked face of the cliff. Dawes swung dizzyingly back and forth as they rose. They were climbing the unvegetated rock as if it were a ladder, and with each new upward thrust he canted out over the emptiness, wisely refusing to look down.

Then the upwardness ended, just when Dawes thought his mind would snap from the constant danger of the climb, and the aliens proceeded inward. Into a cave of some sort, that appeared to be hewn out of the face of the rock cliff.

Dawes' fertile imagination worked overtime. He pictured strange alien sacrificial rites taking place in this Haggardesque cave. Or vampire bats lurking in the darkness ahead, grateful for the sacrifice being brought to them.

But none of the dire perils he conceived came immediately to pass. The aliens simply left him in the cave. They put him down with surprising gentleness, leaving him to lie in cold, moist sand, turned their backs on him, walked away. In the utter darkness he could see nothing at all.

He sensed other aliens moving about; he thought he could tell them by their ape-like shuffle. He wondered if the whole colony was to be carried off and deposited here in this cave. *The survey team said the planet was uninhabited*, he thought reproachfully. *But Dave Matthews was right after all.*

He thought about the interrupted kiss. Then, about the interrupted wedding night. Then, lastly, about the interrupted colony.

It had been such a brave start; the rearing of the stockade, the coupling off, the bubble-houses. Everything had been giving so well for the infant colony. But trouble had taken less than a day to descend on them.

He sat quietly in the darkness. The sound of sobbing was coming from a point somewhere to his right. As background noise he could hear the gentle murmuring sound of flowing water, as if there were a stream bubbling inside the borders of the cave.

'Who's there?' he asked. 'Who are you?'

'It's Carol. Is that you, Mike?'

Some of his fear ebbed away. At least, he thought, he was not alone!

'Yes. Where are you, Carol?'

'Sitting in sand, someplace. I can't see. What's going to happen to us?'

'I don't know,' Dawes said. 'Don't move. Stay right where you are and I'll try to find you. Damn this darkness, anyway!'

He looked around, trying to gauge the direction from which Carol's voice had come. But he knew that no vector would be accurate in here. The walls of the caves would have a distorting effect.

A voice he recognized as Noonan's broke in, saying, 'Dawes, is that you?'

It came from someplace deeper in the cave, behind him, highlighted by resonating echoes. 'Yes,' Dawes said loudly. 'And Carol's here, too. Anyone else?'

'I am,' said Cherry Thomas.

Her declaration echoed around the cavern. No other voices entered in. Staring unseeingly ahead of him, Dawes waited a moment, then said flatly when the echoes died, 'I guess it's just the four of us, then, up here in this cave. What the hell do they want with us?'

Nobody answered.

Outside the cavern mouth, somewhere to his right, the endless wind whipped around the mountains, whistling, moaning. Dawes shivered. In the darkness he could just barely see his own hand held before his face – and even then he could not really be sure whether or not it was imagination, not actual sight, that had put the image of the hand there. He had never experienced a darkness of such intensity before.

And he saw another darkness more clearly now – the darkness of a life that yanked a person out of his rightful place and threw him onto a strange world, and then when he had begun to carve some meaning and familiarity into the strangeness yanked him out again and tossed him in a windswept cave. He felt very alone, very young, more than a little frightened, just a little sick.

He started to crawl across the cold wet sands that formed the floor of the cave. Evidently the brook he heard ran not too deep under the sand, close enough to the surface to impart a chill, and came bubbling out a few hundred yards deeper in the cave.

No one spoke. There was steady sobbing, but he had little hint of a direction. He had no idea even of how large the cave was.

'Carol! Carol!' he called out.

On hands and knees he groped in the blackness. After minutes of uncertain scurrying, he felt a warm hand graze his, startling him a little. The hand found his wrist and tightened comfortingly.

Blindly he reached out. Arms gathered him in. He almost felt like sobbing, out of gratitude, out of shared terror.

He clung wordlessly to her in the darkness, gripping tight as if the girl were the one real thing in a universe of cobwebbed nightmares. 'Thank God,' he murmured. Then he relaxed, and after a while he slept.

CHAPTER TWELVE

The coming of daylight revealed Carol to him. She was lying near him, a pathetic little bundle sprawled on the sand. She was still asleep, her knees drawn up into her body, her hands tucked under one cheek.

And, off to one side, he saw that Cherry also slept – her clothes disheveled, her bright blonde hair streaming every which way.

His body ached; every muscle throbbed, his bones were chilled by the damp and cold, and he felt a general lassitude, the weariness of a body not yet accustomed to the hard mattress that was the floor of the cave.

Noonan was awake already. Dawes saw him far back in the cavern, over to the left on the side away from Carol. He was sitting up, arms clasped in front of him across his knees, looking amusedly at Dawes. With one easy gesture Noonan pushed himself to his feet and ambled down the cavern toward Dawes, who stood waiting.

'These women will sleep through anything,' Noonan chuckled. His eyes narrowed as he saw Dawes more closely. 'Christ, you look awful. Green in the face.'

'I'm – pretty tired out.'

'You getting sick?'

Dawes shook his head. 'I just feel washed out.'

'You look sicker than just being washed out.'

'How am I supposed to feel?' Dawes demanded. 'Who knows where the hell we are? What are these aliens planning to do to us? We may be stew by lunchtime,

Noonan', Dawes' voice sounded thin and high in his ears.

'I doubt it,' Noonan said casually. 'But let's take a look.'

Together they strolled forward to the lip of the cavern. Dawes gasped.

They were at least a hundred feet above the flat, dull-brown surface of Osiris. The cave was inset in an almost vertical rise of cliff. Above and below them were flat walls of black stone, gleaming faintly in the morning sun. And down below, on the distant ground, a few of the aliens moved in aimless patterns as if standing guard.

Dawes pointed out past the thickly forested area. 'Look there. That must be the colony, in that clearing all the way out there!'

Noonan nodded. 'A good ten miles or so. And we can see it easily. This is the damnedest flat world I ever saw, except for these cliffs.' He gestured downward, at the aliens. 'Nasty bunch down there.'

Dawes looked out and down. The aliens, at this distance, appeared to be nothing but yellow-brown splotches against the deeper brown of the soil. They were heavily furred, he saw, neckless, thick-bodied. He thought he could make out the bluish-purpleness of the suction-pads on the palms of their broad hands.

Dawes stepped back from the rim of the cave mouth, remarking with a levity he hardly felt, 'It's a long drop.'

He glanced at the bigger man, who grinned and said, 'Damned right it is. I'd say we were stuck here a while. We'll just have to make the most of it.'

Dawes nodded bleakly and turned away, to survey the interior of the cave.

The cavern was long and deep, deeper than it was wide; it slanted back downward, vanishing into a wall of rock at the rear beyond the penetrating range of the sunlight. Far to the back of the cave the little stream gushed forth out of the live rock, coursed along the cave floor for a space, and dropped below the surface again, puddling up into a small fast-flowing narrow lake. The morning air was cold and brisk; the wind wailed past the open mouth of the cavern in relentless pursuit of itself.

They were a hundred fifty feet above ground, in a cold little alcove in the side of a steep cliff. They had fresh water. They could survive here indefinitely, if—

Hunger gnawed at Dawes' middle. He said to Noonan, 'Suppose we're left here to starve to death? What if they don't bring us food?'

'We'll eat each other,' Noonan said amiably. 'Women and children first.' He yawned, showing sharp, strong white teeth, and Dawes half thought he might be serious. There was never any telling what idea Noonan might put forth as a serious suggestion.

Yet he was glad Noonan was here. The older man radiated strength and competence and courage, all of them attributes that Dawes knew he himself conspicuously lacked. Noonan was an adventurer. He had been a volunteer. That took a kind of courage Dawes could hardly begin to understand, and he respected Noonan for it.

'Let's go wake up the womenfolk,' Noonan suggested.

'We might as well,' Dawes agreed.

He headed to the back of the cavern, where Carol slept. Looking back, he saw Noonan stooping over Cherry, shaking her urgently from side to side.

Carol still lay curled up in a ball-like position. She seemed so soundly asleep that Dawes regretted having to wake her. He knelt by her side, listening for a moment to the untroubled rhythm of her breathing, and wondered how she could be so calmly asleep in a place like this.

He put his hand lightly to her shoulder. 'Carol. Wake up, Carol.'

She stirred, but her eyes remained shut – as if she did not want to wake, Dawes thought; as if she preferred the security of her dream. He shook her more energetically, and she began to awaken. 'Carol? Are you up?'

'What – oh – Mama, yes – I must have overslept—'

Her eyes opened and she sat up. For an instant she stared at Dawes, at the cave, with blank incomprehension. Then her dream of home faded and reality returned.

'Oh – I was dreaming. I slept so soundly all night. I thought you were going to come to me, but you didn't, did you? You—'

'Come,' he said quietly. 'Let's go down to the others. It's morning.'

Cherry had awakened by this time; she stood stretching, knuckling her eyes, adjusting her clothing. Noonan, nearby, stood with arms folded. Dawes and Carol went toward them, and Cherry nodded at Carol, smiled at Dawes. For a long moment the four of them stood apart and looked at each other. Just looked. And Dawes saw suddenly that life in the cave was going to be complicated.

'We're not going to have much privacy in here,' Noonan said at last, breaking a silence so taut it creaked.

'You can say that again,' Cherry offered.

'I won't. But some of us are going to have to change their ideas a little. And I don't know how long we're going to be stuck up here, either – but I'd guess we don't get out until someone *gets* us out.'

'You don't figure there's any way we can get out ourselves?' Dawes asked.

Noonan hunched his shoulders into a somber shrug. 'I don't have any snap ideas. It's a long way down, that's all.'

'Those aliens,' Carol said in a hesitant voice. 'They're down there just *watching* us?'

Noonan nodded. 'There's a bunch of them outside, in the valley at the foot of the cliff. We're penned up here, and they can come get us any time they want. But we can't get out.'

'And I don't suppose the colony is going to come rescue us,' Cherry Thomas said. 'They won't give much of a damn about us. Chalk us off as lost, I guess. They'll be too busy defending their stockade.'

'There isn't any defense,' Carol said. 'If they can walk up the side of a cliff, they can climb over a twenty foot fence, can't they?'

Dawes said, 'The colonists won't rescue us. They *can't*. They don't even know where we are. If there still *is* a colony, that is.'

Noonan shook his head in agreement. 'That's a point. The aliens may have everybody cooped up, four to a cave. Or they may have just snatched the four of us. There's no way of telling.'

'Well, we're stuck here,' Cherry said. 'But what are we going to do about food?'

Noonan shrugged. 'We can't eat sand. Maybe the aliens will be nice about it and bring us something we *can* eat. Or maybe they won't.'

'Suppose they don't?' Carol asked.

'Then there are three things we can do. We can sit around in here and wait to starve to death, or we can take turns eating each other, or we can simply jump out the front of the cave.' Noonan laughed cavernously. 'I'd recommend the last idea. It makes for a quicker death, that way.'

That put a finish to conversation for a while. The four prisoners separated; Noonan stretched out to sleep, Cherry headed to the back of the cave to try the drinking-water, and Carol let herself sink down crosslegged to stare hopelessly at the front of the cave.

The morning slipped by. It was getting close to noon, Dawes figured, and he was awfully hungry. The wind had not let up its furious keening, and the sun was high overhead. He felt too dismal to say anything to anyone.

After a while he walked to the lip of the cavern and peered down the vertiginous height. He was stunned to see alien faces peering upward at him. There were about twenty of the aliens halfway up the side of the cliff, making no attempt to move closer, looking upward at him. Their blunt heads were almost entirely covered with short bristly yellow-brown fur, from which dark blue eyes, piercingly intense, stared out.

Dawes turned away. Suddenly, he heard a thump behind him.

Surprised, he whirled and caught a glimpse of the purple suction-pad of an alien as it flashed and disappeared. A bundle lay at the mouth of the cave. Dawes ran to the edge of the cave and looked out. An alien was scampering down the side of the cliff to rejoin his fellows below.

Dawes returned to the bundle. It was a package about the size of a man, wrapped in a reddish-yellow animal hide that was shaggy and rank. Frowning, Dawes undid the coarse twine that held the uncured hide together and lay back the wrapping.

His eyes widened. Rising, he cupped one hand to his mouth and called out to the others.

'Hey, *food!* Come here, all of you! The aliens brought us food!'

As Noonan and Cherry and Carol came crowding around to see, Dawes spread out the provisions. The largest item in the bundle was a freshly-killed animal, small, foreshortened, vaguely pig-like, with a hairless black skin. A stiff little tail about six inches long thrust out sharply at them. There was a deep gash in the animal's throat, but otherwise it was whole, from its tail to its flattened snout and glassy yellow buttons of eyes. Strapped to the beast by a crude length of twine was a short, sharp knife made of some shiny gray material very much like obsidian.

The bundle also included several clusters of milk-white fruits the size of large grapes, and some oblong blue gourd-like vegetables with coarse, knobby skins. Dawes' mouth watered.

'So it looks like they intend to feed us,' Noonan said. 'That may be good, or maybe it isn't. I hope they're not fattening us for a sacrifice.'

'We'll find that out soon enough,' said Dawes. 'We'll know whenever we get fed again. If they don't throw us any more for a week, we can figure that the fattening idea is wrong.'

'How did the bundle get here?' Cherry asked.

'An alien climbed up the side of the cliff and tossed it in the entrance,' Dawes said. 'Then he beat it. He looked like a big brown spider skittering down the rock wall.'

Using the blade, Noonan sliced into the animal, while Dawes and the women watched. Dawes was fascinated with Noonan's surgical precision. The roughly flaked stone knife was razor sharp, and the big man had a ready way with the beast; he carved with the skill of a professional butcher. He laid the animal open speedily, pulling back flaps of its dark red underbelly skin, and scooped out the warm entrails. He dumped them to one side; they were slimy, oozing with blood.

'At least,' Noonan said, 'the alien blood is the right color.' He efficiently carved chunks of meat from the small creature. 'Maybe this meat is poison and maybe it isn't, but at least the blood's right.'

Carol shuddered. 'I've never eaten raw meat. Isn't there some way we can make a fire?'

Noonan paused to glance up at her. 'No, there isn't,' he said emphatically, 'I know you didn't want to come on this trip, girlie. But you're here, now. You'd better be ready to eat plenty of raw meat – and worse things.'

CHAPTER THIRTEEN

They ate, and it was a strange, silent, almost shame-faced meal. The veneer of civilization that still clung to all of them, even Noonan, dampened their spirits as they ate the bloody meat.

Dawes was voraciously hungry, and it wasn't as hard for him to overcome his conditioning against eating raw meat as he thought it would be. Still, something about the sticky blood that ran between his fingers, pasting them together, made him queasy. And he could see that Carol had to make a visible effort to choke the meat down. Noonan ate without inhibitions. Cherry put away her share with a certain reserve, but with no outward show of revulsion. The meat had an odd, pungent taste about it, even raw, that made it more appealing than it might otherwise have been.

There were ten of the blue gourds. After the meat course, Noonan doled out one gourd to each of them and put the remaining six aside. 'In case we don't get fed again too soon,' he explained. 'These things will keep. The meat won't.'

The gourds tasted sour, strongly acidified; they had a stringy, unpleasant texture, and needed plenty of chewing. But they were nourishing, and filled up the stomach well. Dawes finished his gourd quickly and turned his attention to the white grapes. These were doughy in consistency, dry, and not very good.

When everyone was through eating, Noonan gathered

together the remnants of the meal, the bones of the small animal and the shells of the gourds, and hurled them from the cave mouth. After a distinct pause came the thudding sounds of landing.

'Why'd you do that?' Dawes asked.

'To show them that we appreciated the stuff. There's no better way than to toss back a carcass that's been cleaned of flesh. Anyway, we can't have that junk sitting around in here. Bad for sanitation.'

Cherry Thomas grinned uneasily. 'Sanitation. Glad you brought that matter up. This hotel don't have such good furnishings.'

'We'll set up a couple of latrines up here near the cave-mouth,' Noonan said. 'Better ventilation that way. All the comforts of home.'

'What's a latrine?' Carol asked.

'It's a hole in the ground, dearie.' Noonan's voice dripped concentrated H_2SO_4. 'Just a hole in the ground, that's all. You use it. We can have one for the menfolk, one for womenfolk, if you like.'

'Oh. I see,' Carol said in a small, unhappy voice.

Cherry Thomas giggled in her cold, tinkling way. Noonan rumbled with laughter. Dawes felt profoundly embarrassed for Carol, but said nothing.

Noonan pointed upcavern, where the little stream split the cavern floor into two roughly equal sectors.

'Look here, Dawes. Suppose you and Carol take the far corner up there, on the right.'

'And you?'

'Cherry and I'll stay on the left, a little ways lower down toward the cave mouth. That's for sleeping. It's the best arrangement we can make.'

'It'll be something like living in a goldfish bowl,' Cherry said.

Dawes shrugged. 'We'll have to manage.'

He rose, walked to the front of the cave, and peered out. Seven or eight aliens squatted on the ground a hundred and fifty feet below, looking up.

'More like a goldfish bowl than you think,' he said, turning around. 'They're watching us from down there. Just *watching*. As if – as if we were really fish in a bowl, or pets in a cage.'

'Maybe we are,' Noonan said. He scooped up a handful of moist sand, compressed it in his clenched fist until it was a hard ball, and angrily hurled it down at the staring aliens. It broke apart in midflight and showered harmlessly down as a spray of sand. Noonan turned away, cursing softly.

The day dragged along horribly. Four people in an escape-proof cell a hundred yards long and perhaps seventy feet wide, without fire, without anything but themselves. And they hadn't yet learned to like each other much.

Dawes felt his nerves tightening like the tuned strings of a fiddle. There was nothing to do in the cave but stare at each other, talk, tell jokes. And there was so little to talk about. Noonan was monolithic; he spoke only when he chose, never speaking just for the mere sake of making noise. Carol's conversation seemed to be limited to expressions of faint hopes and fears; Cherry's, to jokes and reminiscences of show business.

Dawes found little to say himself, and spent the hours staring broodingly at his muddy feet. There was no telling how long they would have to stay here, but he saw already that however long it would be, it was going to be hellish.

Cherry had launched into an interminable monologue about her life and good times. It went on for nearly half an hour, as she told the unlistening trio of her happy days under the management of Dan Cirillo, a saint of a man if Cherry's account had any truth to it. She was working up slowly to the great tragedy in her life, when Dan had been selected, leaving her rudderless. But it was taking her a long time to that point.

'So I opened at the Lido on the 24th,' she said. 'Dan got me a great contract – three thousand a week, all the extras I could think of. Ninety-piece orchestra plus synthesizer accompaniment. And me in an evening gown that cost ten grand. I wish I had that evening gown now. I wish I was back there in Nevada. I wish I was anywhere, anywhere but in this lousy cave.'

The monologue came to a temporary halt. In the silence Carol said, in a dead, flat voice, 'We aren't going to get out. I know we aren't. Not ever. We're just going to stay here and rot. There are times I feel like just jumping out and—'

'Carol!' Dawes burst out.

The girl looked up at him without understanding. Her eyes were glazed with fatigue and fear.

After a shocked little pause Cherry said, 'Well, the kid's got a point there. We're stuck in here for good. If I'd known what was good for me, I would have gone with Dan back in '14, and we'd be together somewhere having kids, instead of me being stuck here in this lousy cave where we can't even—'

'That's enough, Cherry,' Noonan interrupted. 'Stop moaning about what you didn't do in '14. What's past is past.'

'So we'll rot away here and—'

'*That's enough, Cherry!*' Noonan snapped to his feet out of a crosslegged position without using his hands. 'I've got an idea,' he said. 'Maybe it isn't worth much, but at least I can try it.'

He began to strip off his shirt, kicking off his shoes at the same time.

'What are you going to do?' Dawes asked.

Noonan unsnapped his trousers. 'Take a look at that underground stream up back. I'm going to get in there and wander around a little. Maybe the stream comes out somewhere. Maybe we can all get out the other side.'

He picked up his clothes, stuffed them under his arm, and, wearing only briefs, walked upcavern to the place where the stream broke the surface of the cavern floor. Looking back he called, 'Come on up here with me, Dawes. If you hear me yell, come on in after me.'

Dawes joined him. Noonan tossed down the bundle of his clothes, and entered the water. It swirled knee-deep as he waded farther upcavern, then abruptly grew deeper.

As it approached the height of his chest, Dawes said uneasily, 'It's dangerous to try this, Noonan. You may get trapped underneath, somewhere. I won't be able to hear you if you yell.'

Noonan turned to glance back. His lips were blue, and despite himself he was shivering, but he smiled. 'So? What of it? At least I tried.'

He turned again and advanced toward the point at which the stream dipped below ground level again and swept back into the mountain. Dawes heard Noonan suck breath in gaspingly, and then Noonan went under. Tensely Dawes began to count off the seconds.

A thousand one, a thousand two, a thousand three, a thousand four . . .

A thousand six, a thousand seven . . .

. . . a thousand ten . . .

'Where did he go?' Dawes heard Cherry ask.

He turned and saw both women standing behind him.

'He went under,' Dawes said simply.

Thousand fifteen . . . thousand sixteen . . . thousand seventeen . . .

. . . thousand twenty . . .

... thousand twenty-five ...

'He's been gone half a minute,' Dawes said a few seconds later. 'He ought to be up soon.'

'Suppose he doesn't come up?' Carol asked.

Dawes did not answer. But he kicked off his shoes, knowing he'd be expected to go in after Noonan and try to find him. He started to shiver a little, and his hands went tentatively to his belt.

... thousand thirty-six. How long could a man stay under water? Even a man like Noonan?

'You oughta go in and look for him,' Cherry said. 'He may be drowning.'

'Yeah. I know.'

... thousand forty ...

The counting mechanism in his mind was functioning automatically now, ticking away the seconds. *Thousand forty-two.* With a cold hand Dawes started to strip off his trousers, not worrying about modesty in the face of the cold stream that awaited him.

Suddenly Noonan broke surface, head first – leaping up high above the water, gasping loudly for breath, plunging back down like a sounding whale.

Choking, retching, he came up again, battled the swift current for an instant or two, and managed to pull himself to the edge of the water. Dawes waded in a couple of feet, grabbed his arm, and tugged him up on the sand.

Noonan was blue all over; goosebumps of enormous size covered him. He lay there, sprawled out with his face down in the sand, drawing in breath with great hoarse sobbing sighs. Finally he looked up.

'Cold,' he said. '*Cold!*'

'You find anything?' Dawes asked.

Weakly Noonan shook his head. 'No. Not a damned thing. I followed the stream as far as I could. Nothing. Came back and couldn't find the outlet. Thought I'd –

thought I'd drown. Then I broke through.'

He shivered convulsively. Dawes had never seen a man look so cold and completely exhausted before. Noonan continued to sob for breath.

'He'll freeze to death,' Carol said anxiously. 'He's all wet and the sand's sticking to him. We ought to warm him up somehow.'

Dawes felt irritated by her show of sympathy. Noonan's wild swim, he thought, had been nothing but a grandstand play; showboating for the benefit of the women, and nothing more.

'He'll warm up by himself,' Dawes grunted.

Cherry glared at him. 'The hell he will. You leave him like that, he'll catch pneumonia or something. But I'll take care of him.'

Dawes looked at her, startled.

Cherry lay down in the sand next to the still gasping Noonan. She put her arms around him.

'You two go away,' she said without looking up. 'I'll keep my husband warm.'

Dawes and Carol walked toward the cave mouth without looking back. He was angry and depressed. Noonan's show of heroism had made its effect. And what had Noonan hoped to gain? To find an underwater passageway through the mountain and out the other side? That was clearly impossible. Noonan had just wanted to flex his muscles, to get some exercise, and, almost incidentally, to prove unnecessarily that he was a real man, not a skinny imitation of one.

And Carol had been impressed. Dawes had seen it in her eyes, as she took in the sight of the exhausted Noonan sprawled heroically in the sand. Dawes was more than ever conscious of his callowness now.

Later, as the big sun dipped toward night, Noonan recovered from his exertions, dressed, and he and Cherry joined Dawes and Carol at the cave mouth. The four of them sat at the cavemouth, together and not together. Dawes sensed conflict growing among them. Noonan still looked a little the worse for his swim. Dawes sat with his arms around Carol, and she made no objection, possibly because of the warmth his nearness provided.

No more food had come that day. The aliens obviously planned to give them just one meal a day – if that.

'We need a hostage,' Noonan said, talking more to himself than to any of the others. 'It's the only way to get anywhere. Tomorrow we hang around the cave mouth until they bring the food – *if* they bring the food. When the alien shows up, we grab him.'

'What good is that going to do?' Dawes wanted to know.

'I don't know,' Noonan said. 'But at least it's *something*, dammit! A sign that we're doing something to get out. You want to sit on your can in here forever, kid?'

'We probably will,' said Cherry. 'Like goddam pets. Birds in a gilded cage. Why couldn't those apes have picked someone else? Why us?'

Night was falling. Outside, in the valley, a red alien bonfire flickered.

'They're watching us,' Dawes said. 'Watching all the time. They want to see what we'll do. They want to see how long it takes before we start fighting, before we hate each other's guts, before we start jumping off this damned cliff to get free.'

'Shut up,' Noonan snapped.

Dawes ignored him. 'I mean it! It's like a lab experiment. I had experiments like this is psych class, in college. You take four rats, see, and you stick them in a cage. Or you put them on a treadmill, and toss them some food when they look bushed. That's what we are, rats on a treadmill. The experimenter waits and watches, taking notes, looking to see how long it is until the rats start snapping at each other, until they drop from exhaustion.'

'I told you to shut up,' Noonan rumbled threateningly.

'Who the hell are you to tell me anything?'

Noonan got up and clamped one heavy hand down on Dawes' shoulder. 'Look, kid, we all know life's tough in here. Don't make it any tougher. Quite whining or I'll toss you out the cave mouth myself.'

'Yeah,' Dawes shot back at him. 'You like to get rid of me. What a nice setup that would be, just you and the two girls in here—'

Noonan slapped him, hard.

Dawes took the stinging blow the wrong way, neck held rigid, and it nearly broke him in two. After a moment, when he regained his wits, he said softly, 'Sorry, Noonan. I didn't mean to rile you.'

'Okay, kid. Just sit there and shut up.'

'But you see it, don't you? We're doing just what the aliens want! They want to see which one of us cracks first, and how he does it! They want to see us fight. They want to see us tear each other apart.'

'They're just primitive savages sitting round a bonfire,' Noonan said derisively. 'You're making things up. Giving us all that college stuff. You're making up things that don't exist.'

'Maybe. Maybe I am,' Dawes said. There was sudden tension in the cavern. The two women were silent. Dawes looked at Noonan, and licked away the salty dribble of blood on his lip. 'I tell you they're just waiting to see us crack up.'

'Well, we won't give 'em the satisfaction. We can hold out. Remember the speech they made at Bangor. We're *Earthmen*. The galaxy's finest.' Noonan looked toward the cave mouth. 'Damned moonless planet,' he muttered.

'No light out there at all. But we'll beat them, though. I tell you that.'

'Don't kid yourself, Noonan,' said Cherry, half to herself. 'The crack-up's coming. It won't take long.'

CHAPTER FOURTEEN

In the darkness of that second night, Dawes cradled Carol in his arms. Noonan and Cherry had settled down for the night somewhere downcavern. In the utter darkness, there was no knowing where.

Carol was warm, pliable, with tense reserve of tight-strung nervousness. They were silent a long while, holding each other for warmth.

After a while the girl said, 'How long can we stay living like this? The four of us. I thought you and Noonan were going to fight today, when he told you to shut up and slapped you.'

'Noonan can kill me with his pinky and thumb. It wouldn't have been much of a fight. But I was asking for it. I started to crack up.'

She pressed suddenly hard against him. He wished he could see her face. He would have liked to know whether she looked sympathetic or merely scornful, pitying.

In three days, Dawes was beginning to think that cave life might almost become bearable. It was possible for human beings to adapt to almost any kind of situation, he told himself. Even living in a cold, windy cave on an alien planet.

Food came regularly, about noon each day – the same assortment each time: a newly-killed beast, white grapes, gourds. Noonan's plan of catching an alien and holding him as a hostage proved about as practicable as flying out of the cave, or walking insectlike down the sheer face of the cliff. Each day the alien messenger would fling the food package into the cave and vanish before the watching men could move. They kept guard for two days, but without even coming close to success. The alien would climb the cliff, hurl the bundle in, and scamper away again. After two days Noonan and Dawes completely abandoned the idea of being able to catch one.

But, Dawes decided, you could get used to anything. You could get used to slimy raw meat dripping with blood, to grapes that weren't grapes, to a latrine dug in the sand and to living without soap or depilator or any of the other pretty things of civilization. There were no mirrors – the stream flowed too fast, and the back of the cave was too dark for it to serve – and without mirrors a lot can be overlooked. A tacit understanding not to discuss anyone else's appearance sprang up; Dawes was happy about it. He saw the stubble sprouting on Noonan's face and the blotches on Cherry's, and knew that he probably looked equally unkempt.

When you live in a goldfish bowl, Dawes thought, you don't waggle fingers at the other goldfish and loudly cry holier-than-thou. There was no percentage in it.

Dawes was able to persuade himself that it was going to be all right, that the four of them would be able to work out a living pattern involving minimum friction, that would endure for however longer their imprisonment continued. But he soon found out how wrong he was.

The aliens were keeping constant watch. They gave no hint of their motives, but milled about ceaselessly in the valley, and occasionally came skittering past the cave mouth for a quick peek in.

And, though the four humans tried to prevent it from

happening, tension mounted in the cave. It had to. Civilization didn't wash off as easily as all that.

It began with little things – little trivial wormlike bickerings between them. One time, Noonan objected when Dawes took the largest share of that day's meat for himself, after Noonan had carved the still warm carcass into four rough chunks that were not quite equal.

'Why don't you wait till I hand the stuff out?' Noonan asked.

'Because I'm hungry.'

'I wanted that piece for myself.'

'Why should you get it?'

'I carved,' Noonan said. 'And I'm the biggest. I need the most food.'

They snarled at each other for a second more; then Cherry suggested that they trim a little of the meat from the big piece and add it to one of the other portions, and Dawes nodded. The tension died away. But the dispute was part of the pattern.

And there was the time when Cherry was halfway through her account of the perils of show business for the third time; having reached the point in her autobiography that dealt with Dan's selection, and being unwilling to talk in any great detail about the segment of her life that had followed that event, Cherry had backtracked and was reciting her early struggles once again.

Carol waited patiently until Cherry launched into a by-now-familiar graphic description of how a lecherous old nightclub owner had forced her to submit to a casting-couch routine before he would give her a contract. 'So he backed me into a corner and I could see him starting to drool over me,' Cherry said, 'and I told him, "Look here, Mr. Fletcher, if you think you're going to—"'

Suddenly Carol burst out, with vehemence that was

unusual for her, 'How often are you going to tell that filthy story? I'm sick and tired of it!'

'You don't like my stories, go somewhere. All we got to do in this place is talk. So I'm talking. It makes me happy. I know I'm still alive when I talk.'

'You don't have to keep talking the same thing all the time!'

'What else am I gonna talk about? These things *happened* to me! They *are* me! Just because you're jealous, because you spent your whole silly little life doing what other people told you to do and never getting any enjoyment out of your stupid life—'

'You can't talk about me like that!' Carol screeched.

They yelled back and forth at each other for a minute or two more, and next thing the argument exploded into a fight, the two women springing at each other and rolling over and over in a tangle of arms and legs, pulling hair, screaming, shouting. Noonan and Dawes had been at the other end of the cave; they came on the run and dragged them apart. Carol had been on top, pounding Cherry's head against the sand, when they were pulled apart.

The winds wailed. Cherry and Carol glowered at each other; then, as Noonan shoved Cherry toward the other girl, they reluctantly shook hands. Dawes looked out into the valley. The aliens outside had increased in number; there were twenty or thirty of them now. They seemed to be enjoying the spectacle in the cave.

The next incident came on the fourth day, when Dawes and Carol were bathing. Carol was at the water's edge, cupping up handfuls and rubbing her face and body to break the shock of climbing in. A sort of convention had sprung up in the cave – when one couple bathed, the other busied themselves elsewhere, to provide at least the impression of privacy. But as he prepared to undress and join Carol in the water, Dawes glanced around and saw Noonan leaning against the cave wall not far from the mouth, watching them.

For a surprised second or two, Dawes had no idea of what to say. The convention in the cave had always been a completely unspoken one, and he knew Noonan cared very little about his own privacy or anybody else's. But still, thought Dawes, in angry annoyance, there was such a thing as common decency, even here in the cave.

While he stared silently at Noonan, the big man smiled coldly and said, 'Something wrong?'

'What are you looking at?' Dawes demanded.

'You want me to tell you?'

'Just suppose you keep your eyes where they belong!' Dawes was angered by the big man's casual amorality. It was just as easy for Noonan to look the other way and avoid such frictions.

'Mike,' Carol whispered warningly. 'Don't make trouble with him. Don't start a ruckus. Why can't you just ignore him?'

'No,' he said. 'There are some things you just don't do. He isn't going to get away with this.'

He became uncomfortably aware of Cherry's mocking eyes on him, and Noonan's. Carol stood at the water's edge with her hands uncertainly shielding her body from view. 'Get into the water,' he ordered the girl brusquely. 'I don't want him looking at you that way.'

Silently, she obeyed him. Dawes walked downcavern to where Noonan waited, still leaning against the wall. The older man seemed to tower two or three feet above him, even leaning.

Dawes said sharply, 'Are you trying to make it worse in here? You didn't have to look at her that way. There was no call for that.'

'I'll put my eyes wherever I damned please, sonny-

140

boy. And I'm tired of your niceness. This isn't any private hotel we got here.'

'You don't have to go out of your way to make life tough here,' Dawes returned. 'I don't want you watching Carol when we bathe, from now on, Noonan. Do you understand that? We can at least *pretend* we're civilized – even if some of us don't happen to be.'

Noonan hit him. This time, Dawes expected the blow, and was ready for it. He rolled agilely to one side and in the same motion directed an open-handed slap at Noonan's face.

The big man took it like the brush of a gnat's wing, laughed, and tapped Dawes sharply in the pit of the stomach. Dawes felt his knees start to buckle. He caught himself, sucked in his breath.

He swung wildly at Noonan, missed his face by a foot, and swung again. This time Noonan opened one big hand, grabbed Dawes' flailing arm, and twisted it.

Yelling, Dawes tried to break loose. He succeeded in clawing at Noonan's throat with his free arm, distracting the big man's attention for a moment. Dawes ripped loose from Noonan. He danced back a couple of feet, panting, feeling the excitement of combat even though he knew he was yet to score a telling point in the contest.

He darted forward and flicked out a fist. Noonan clubbed his hand aside, stepped forward, hit Dawes almost gently on the point of his right shoulder. The impact stunned him; he felt the surge of pain ripple down his arm to his fingers. Desperately he tried to land a blow, but once again Noonan caught his wrist.

This time there was no breaking loose. Noonan inexorably forced him to the ground.

'I'm gonna put my eyes wherever I please,' Noonan said quietly. There was no malice in his voice, nor anger; just a level affirmation of victory. 'You hear that, Dawes?

You ain't giving any orders inside here. If I want to look at your girl, I'll look at her, and you ain't gonna tell me I can't do it. Understand that, Dawes?'

'For God's sake, Noonan – act like a human being,' Dawes whispered harshly.

As if in answer, Noonan tucked both of Dawes' wrists in one massive paw and slapped him a few times with the other, until Dawes' head reeled.

Cherry said, 'That's enough, Ky. He's only a kid. You want to kill him?'

'I want to show him he can't go telling Ky Noonan what to do!'

The big hand ground Dawes' wrists together, while the other descended, whack-whack, quick stunning backhand and forehand blows across Dawes' cheeks. Finally Noonan tired of the sport. He released Dawes, scooping him up and throwing him sprawling back upcavern.

'You didn't need to do that to him, Ky,' Cherry said reproachfully.

'Shut up!' Noonan snarled. 'You trying to tell me what I should do, too?'

Dawes lay where he had fallen, not making any effort to get up. His wrists ached painfully where Noonan's grip had pressed them together, and his cheeks were raw and hot, partly out of shame and partly from the impact of Noonan's angry blows. He hadn't even stood a chance in the fight. It was worse than Don Quixote tilting off at windmills; Noonan could have killed him with two swings of his arm.

Carol had remained upcavern by the stream during the entire fight. Now she came over to him. She looked down at him without speaking, without smiling, without offering a word of sympathy. Dawes could not tell whether the grave look in her eyes was one of pity or of contempt.

After a while she walked away, back to the stream, and began to dress.

Dawes elbowed himself to a sitting position and massaged his wrists. Downcavern he saw that Noonan had stretched out for a nap. Cherry was drawing sketches in the sand. The cave was very silent.

He walked slowly back to the stream, knelt by it, and sloshed water over his face; the shock of the sudden coldness eased some of the pain of Noonan's slaps. Shaking himself dry, Dawes went downcavern, past Cherry and Noonan, to stare out of the mouth of the cave. The clearing below was packed with aliens. He wondered if they had enjoyed the performance.

CHAPTER FIFTEEN

After that, there was a strange realignment of the tense relationships between the four prisoners in the cave. The incident of the beating was a sort of dividing-point, separating what had been from what now was.

Dawes suffered the most; he had acted foolishly, rashly, in deliberately inviting Noonan to trounce him, and he had lost status in Carol's eyes. That was clear. The only sort of respect she could have for him would be based on his intelligence – and he hadn't acted intelligently toward Noonan. Further, Carol really wanted a man who could take care of her, who could protect her from the tensions and rigors of existence in a frightening world – and Dawes had not at all proved himself that kind of person.

But sympathy came from an unexpected quarter - from Cherry, who glared at the invincibly self-sufficient Noonan, and offered soothing words to Dawes. Noonan glared back at her angrily. His possessiveness was obviously beginning to irritate Cherry. Dawes wondered when the open split between them would come.

The swirl of conflicting emotions tightened. Both women half-loved and half-pitied Dawes. Cherry was physically drawn to Noonan, but was repelled by his dominating ways, his assertion of ownership. Noonan claimed Cherry as his own property, but quite clearly he was interested in Carol as well. Around and around it went, while the aliens gathered outside, and the hours slid to-

ward sundown and the moonless darkness of Osiris'
night.

Dawes sat bitterly by himself, feeling that he had fallen into total disgrace. Cherry softly sang her old night-
club songs, muffling their stridencies to avoid touching
off some new dispute in the cave. Carol did nothing. As
for Noonan, he bathed, slept for a while, woke, and went
to the front of the cave, flattening himself strangely at
the mouth, poking his head out and staring down for a
long time as if measuring some distance.

After a time he came back and spoke with Cherry for
a few moments. Then, moving on, he went to Carol as she
sat quietly against the cave wall, and nudged her.

Dawes glanced up from his brooding. Noonan was saying something to her. He strained his ears to catch their
words; but the expression on Noonan's face told him all
he really needed to know.

Cherry crossed the cave, taking a seat at Dawes' side
and putting her hand on his wrist as he began to clench
his fists.

'Don't pay any attention to it,' she murmured. 'It was
bound to happen sooner or later. Don't make him have
to hit you again.'

'Is she going to listen to him?'

Cherry shrugged. 'I don't know. But she may. You
never can tell.'

'I hate him,' Dawes said darkly. 'I hate both of them.
If he wasn't twice my size—'

'Well, he is,' Cherry said. 'So you might as well just
relax.'

She shook out her long blonde hair. It was getting
stringy from lack of combing, and it seemed to Dawes
that it was darkening at the roots. It didn't surprise him
much to find that Cherry's blondeness was synthetic.

He tried to relax, to ignore the fact that elsewhere in

the cave Noonan was successfully taking Carol away from him.

After a long silence Cherry said, 'You know, Noonan thinks he knows a way out of here.'

'*What?*'

'Shh. He told me about it just a while ago. He says there's a little ledge down the side of the cliff a way. Thinks we could manage to reach it with a rope ladder made out of our clothes. But he won't say anything about it to you because he doesn't want to help you.'

Dawes scowled. 'He's got no right to keep something like that to himself—'

'Noonan never worries about rights. Besides, he doesn't really think his idea could work. We might be able to get down, all right, but then the aliens would just bring us right back up here.'

Dawes had to acknowledge the truth of that. He slumped back, the momentary spark of hope dying. The waiting jailers below would never let them escape so openly, he thought.

Shadows deepened in the cave as the angle of sunlight sharpened. Four days, Dawes thought leadenly. Four days of just Noonan and Carol and Cherry, and the captivity might well go on forever. Forever. Was this why he had been selected and flung out into space, to sit in a cave with three other people, guarded by aliens for some unfathomable alien reason? He thought of all the vast and cumbersome machinery of selection, the computer and the local boards and the blue letter from District Chairman Mulholland, whoever *he* might be, damn his politicking hide! District Chairman Mulholland, Dawes thought, was probably some boot-licking nonentity who took a sinister delight in packing people off to the other planets. And for what? So they could be captured by ape-things and stuffed into a cave?

A few more days with Noonan and Carol and Cherry and he might easily go out of his mind. Dawes remembered a line from some play he had once seen performed at State: *Hell is other people.*

Whoever wrote that line had been right, he thought. Carol and Noonan were laughing, there at the back of the cave. Dawes forced himself to sit still. It was hopeless to try to interfere. If Noonan had developed a craving for Carol, there would be no peace in the cave until Noonan had satisfied that craving, and nothing Dawes would do could alter that. He listened numbly to their gay laughter. Carol had never laughed like that in his arms, Dawes thought bitterly.

He knew Cherry was laughing at him, too, inside, laughing because he didn't have the strength to knock Noonan sprawling as he deserved. On the outside, Cherry was pitying him. Inside, laughing.

The sun dropped almost out of sight; no more remained to the day but a few dim red flickers. The eternal wind howled wildly. Dawes looked out into the gathering night, moonless as ever.

'I wonder how the colony's doing,' he said abstractedly. 'Whether they're still there or not. And whether they ever ask themselves what happened to us.'

'You're always *thinking*,' Cherry said. 'Asking yourself questions. Well, the people in the colony don't have time to wonder about us – if they're alive. They're too busy surviving.'

The light went completely. In the dark, Dawes heard Carol's laugh. It sounded strange, harsh, ugly to him. Topping it came the deep chuckle of Noonan.

'The light's out,' Noonan said, loud enough to be heard all over the cave. 'Time to go to bed.'

'Yeah,' said Dawes. 'Time to go to bed.'

He hunched into himself, cradling his head on his

arms, and clenched his eyes tight. Sleep was a long time in coming, and it seemed to him he had hardly fallen off when the first rays of morning were streaming through the narrow mouth of the cave.

Morning. The fifth day.

And the invisible threads of hatred coiled a little tighter around the four in the cave.

Carol was unaccountably red-eyed and sullen. She bathed alone, early. Dawes watched her, from the distance, without getting up. She was like a little child in so many ways – helpless, frightened, selfish.

When Carol was through washing, Noonan bathed, and after him Dawes made his slow way to the rear of the cavern and plunged into the little stream enjoying the sharp pain of the ice-cold water against his skin.

At noon, the food bundle was hurled into the cave right on schedule. They ate silently, Noonan dividing the food as usual and doing a reasonably fair job of it. Not a word had been spoken in the cave since dawn. Dawes looked out and saw the aliens massed below, in greater numbers than ever before. After the meal, he settled into a corner of the cave. Cherry and Carol and Noonan each took up positions far from each other.

Carol. Noonan. Dawes. Cherry. Scattered over the cave like particles which innately repelled each other. No one spoke.

It was Cherry who split the silence finally. 'How long are we supposed to stay like this?' she asked, her voice hard. 'We sit here staring like mortal enemies at each other! Christ, what did we ever *do* to each other that makes us hate this way?'

'Shut up,' Noonan growled.

Carol chuckled hysterically. 'What did we *do*? I'll tell you. We were born, that's what we did to each other. We came into this world and we were picked together and we ended up in this damned cave, making each other miserable.'

'We grate on each other,' Dawes said.

He found himself hating Carol for having gone to Noonan, hating Cherry for her noisy banter, hating Noonan for simply being Noonan. Flimsy reasons, all. But powerful enough to spark the currents of hate in the cave.

'Why can't we get along with each other?' Cherry demanded of no one particular.

'We don't like each other,' Dawes said. 'You'd almost think the aliens picked us that way, to see what would happen when we were penned together. You'd—'

He stopped, suddenly, pushed himself to his feet, walked to the cave mouth, and looked down. As always the height made him a little dizzy, and he gripped the side of the rock for reassurance.

'Yeah, look at them,' he said. 'They sit down there as if they know everything that's happening in this cave. As if they're drinking in all the hatred that's rising between us. As if—'

'Stop that crazy babble,' Noonan ordered brusquely. 'You hurt my ears.'

Dawes knelt and peered down the face of the cliff, trying to see Noonan's ridge. Yes, there it was, a narrow, precipitous shelf of rock projecting no more than a few inches from the cliffside. Turning, Dawes said to Noonan, 'I understand you know how to get us out of here. Why the hell haven't you spoken up about it?'

'Who in blazes told you that? It's not true!'

'The ledge down there,' Cherry said. 'Yesterday you told me—'

Noonan slapped her viciously. Glaring at Dawes, he said, 'Okay, so there's a ledge down there. But my idea won't work, anyway. Even if we got out, the aliens would just grab us and put us right back in the cave. Well, won't they?'

'Maybe not,' Dawes said.

'Maybe not! Maybe not!' Norman roared with laughter. 'You can bet your life they will! You think they'll just sit down there and let us traipse past them?'

'Maybe. I know how to beat the aliens,' Dawes said in a level voice.

Suddenly Carol started to laugh – a high, keening, mad shriek of a laugh, repeated over and over. It wasn't hysteria, but the nearest approach to hysteria. Moments later Cherry was giggling, calmly, cynically.

'Keep quiet!' Dawes shouted. 'Let me talk!'

'We don't want to hear any crazy nonsense out of you,' Noonan snapped. 'Shut your mouth.'

Dawes grinned oddly and took two unhesitant steps forward. There was only one way he could make Noonan listen to him. With careful aim he jabbed the big man sharply in the ribs.

Noonan was astonished by the assault. He glared at Dawes in amazement for an instant, and rumbled into action. His fists shot out blindingly crashing into Dawes' stomach, pounding him under the heart. Dawes fought back grimly. He landed a solid blow on Noonan's lip; then Noonan snarled angrily and cracked him backward with two fast punches in the midsection.

Dawes landed hard, feeling pain lance through his body. He gasped for breath. Noonan stood over him, dispassionately kicked him. Each blow was a new agony.

Finally it was over. Dawes lay crumpled on the ground, shielding his face. Noonan stood over him, and a strange expression of guilt was beginning to cross his features. His lower lip was swelling.

Sitting up, Dawes put his hands to his ribs; nothing was broken. He said hoarsely to Noonan. 'Okay. You were spoiling to kick me around again, and now you did it. You got it all out of your system. I hope you did, anyway.'

Noonan looked completely drained of fight. He didn't speak. Dawes mopped a trickle of blood away from his lips and went on.

'Noonan, you're a strong man, and in some ways you're a clever man. But you couldn't figure a way out of here, and you were damned if you'd let *me* have a go at it without beating me up first. Okay, I got beat up.'

'Listen—' Noonan began unsteadily.

Dawes cut him off. Despite the pain of the beating, he felt a kind of exhilaration. 'You listen to *me*. We can get out of here, if we only cooperate. All four of us.

'I don't know what kind of things those aliens are – but they aren't as primitive as they look. We've been writing them off as ugly ape-things, but they're a lot subtler and smarter than that. I think they grabbed us out of the colony and stuck us up here so they could listen in on our emotions, soak them up, feed on them. They took four of us. Four people who hardly knew one another. They threw us here and left us alone. They knew damned well what would happen. They knew we'd start hating each other, that we'd fight and quarrel and build walls around ourselves. That's what they wanted us to do. It would be a sort of circus for them – a purge, maybe. A kind of entertainment. Okay. They were right. We put on a good show for them. And I'll bet they've been out there drinking up every bit of friction and hate and fighting that's gone on in this cave since we got here.'

Dawes paused. The words were flowing smoothly, now that he had been granted the floor, but he wanted to allow time for his ideas to sink into the other three minds.

'Go on,' Noonan said quietly. 'Finish telling us what you have to say.'

151

'We don't *have* to hate each other, that's what I'm trying to get across. Sure, we get on each others' nerves. Four saints in a cage like this would drive each other batty. But we can turn the hate outward. Hate *them*. And the best way we can show our hate for them is by loving each other instead of fighting. We're playing into their hands by bickering and brawling. Let's work together and try to understand each other. I'll admit up to now I've been as selfish as any of you. We're all equally to blame. But if we start cooperating now – hell, we'll be of no more use to them than fighting cocks without any fight. And we can build that rope ladder and they'll let us go.'

No one spoke when Dawes had finished. He let them think it over, and finally Cherry said, 'They're like parasites, then. Getting their kicks from our hate?'

'You've got the idea.' Dawes looked at the big man. 'Noonan, what do you say? You think what I said is worth anything?'

Slowly, Noonan began to smile despite the swollen lip. 'Yeah. Maybe you've got something. I guess we could try it.'

CHAPTER SIXTEEN

At Dawes' suggestion they relaxed for an hour or so, talking the situation out quietly, before starting to build the rope ladder. Sweating despite the chill, Dawes took charge of the discussion, showing the others as tactfully as he could that there was no real reason for discord in the cave.

Gradually he even began to convince himself. The aliens had made Noonan stare at Carol, had brought on all the humiliation and loss of privacy. And Noonan hadn't really meant to take away Carol last night. He had just been acting out of pique, out of the senseless non-motivation that their confinement provided.

Dawes began to regard the other three as just *people*. He didn't hate Noonan any more, or scatterheaded Carol, or cynical Cherry. They were only people. *Earth* people, frail and imperfect, and they each carried around their own private unhappinesses. In the cave, four sets of desires and weaknesses and selfishnesses had impinged, causing conflict. But now, if each only gave ground a little, harmony could prevail.

And the others began to understand, as Dawes made it plain for them. Slowly, because they were not quick-thinking people, they were starting to grasp the essential truth of their situation. And the tension and distrust and hatred was washing out and draining away.

When they were all smiling, Dawes gently steered the discussion toward the matter of escaping.

He said, 'Noonan, you say we can get out of here if we build a rope ladder of some kind. Will you show us how to build this ladder of yours?'

'We'll build it out of clothes,' Noonan said. 'Obviously. That's the only kind of fabric we have. Let's all start undressing.'

He peeled off his shirt and trousers and tied them together, leg to sleeve, with an elaborate knot. He reinforced it with a sock.

Carol was wearing a skirt. She unfastened it, stepped out of it, and handed it over.

Dawes donated his pants. The line was growing quickly. At Noonan's command Dawes and Cherry roamed the cave collecting the animal hides that the aliens had used to wrap the daily food bundles in. There were four of them. Noonan slashed them into long strips with the obsidian-like knife and added them to the line.

'Okay,' Noonan said at last. 'Maybe this'll do. Let's test it. Dawes, get yourself on the other end of this thing and pull hard.'

Dawes took a double grip on the rope and pulled, as hard as he could, digging his feet into the sand to keep from being dragged toward Noonan. The line held.

'Good,' Noonan grunted. 'She's tight.'

He anchored the end of the line to a jutting rock near the mouth of the cave, hurled the free end out, and let it dangle. Noonan said, 'I'm going to climb down to the ledge. Carol and Cherry will follow me. And then you, Dawes. All clear?'

Noonan grasped the line, tugged it to make sure it was fast, and lowered himself over the edge. Just before he disappeared below the floor level of the cave he grinned, and Dawes grinned back.

'Good luck, Noonan.'

'Thanks. I'll probably need it.'

Dawes watched tensely as Noonan descended, hand under hand, swaying in the wind. He dangled at the very end of the line, his hands grasping the rope only an inch or two from its end, and still his feet scrabbled for purchase, his arms flailed wildly to balance him, and then he stood solid, looking up at them and smiling.

'Okay,' Noonan called. 'Carol. You come down next. Keep your feet clamped to the rope and hold on tight.'

Pale, frightened beyond the point of feeling fear, Carol took hold of the rope. She paused for an instant.

'Go on.' Dawes said softly. 'It's safe. Just hold on and let yourself down hand by hand.'

The girl grasped the rope with her small hands, wrapped her legs round it, and started to descend. Dawes held his breath. The rope seemed tremendously long. Was she going to make it all the way? Or would she fatigue and topple off, still eighty feet above the ground?

She made it. She dangled in mid-air a few feet above Noonan; he stretched out his arms for her, urged her to let go, and finally she did. He caught her and put her safely down on the ledge.

Cherry was next. She showed no outward sign of fear, and she negotiated the descent quickly and skillfully. Dawes waited until she stood by Carol's side on the ledge. Then, taking a last look at the cave, he grabbed hold of the rope himself.

He had done plenty of rope-climbing in high school, in an ultimately fruitless attempt to put some muscle on his skinny body. But those had been fifteen or twenty-foot ropes. This one dangled for a hundred feet, and no protective mat waited beneath it.

Positioning one hand beneath the other, he let himself down, feeling the savage bite of the wind against his skin. He knew the others were waiting for him, watching him, maybe praying. Once, he glanced down, and saw he still had nearly half the distance to go. His muscles were quivering and his arms felt as if they were about to part company with their sockets. But he made it.

He hovered above the shelf and Noonan caught him around the waist and pulled him down to safety. The line swung out over the valley and flapped back against the side of the cliff.

Dawes caught his breath and looked downward from the ledge. 'We're still at least forty feet from the ground. What now?'

'I'm going to try to yank the line loose,' Noonan said. 'All of you hold on to me. If I can pull it down, we tie it on here and climb down to the ground.'

'And if we can't pull it down?' Dawes asked.

Noonan glared for a moment. 'You still haven't lost your old habits. You ask too many damfool questions. Come on – anchor me.'

They held him, while he tugged at the line, grunting bitterly. Muscles corded and bunched along Noonan's back and shoulders, and tendons stood out sharply in the hollow of his elbow. The line was tied too securely at the top, though. It would not come. Noonan pulled harder—

The rope snapped loose with an impact that nearly threw the four of them off the ledge. Noonan looked at the dangling end he held in his hands, then up at the dangling line still fastened at the cavemouth. The rope had snapped in half.

Noonan cursed eloquently. 'I hadn't figured on that. But it could have been worse, I guess.'

'How much rope do we have?' Dawes asked.

'Look for yourself.'

Noonan let the line out over the side of the ledge. It stopped short nearly fifteen feet from the ground. And, Dawes thought, a fifteen-foot jump was an invitation for broken ankles or worse – and they still had a trek of perhaps ten miles back to the colony.

He looked quizzically at Noonan. The big man said, 'We can still manage it. But it's going to take teamwork. *Real* teamwork. I'll go down the rope. Dawes, you follow, go right on down me and hang to my ankles. The girls will do the same, and jump when they reach your ankles. It can't be more than a six or seven-foot drop from there.'

Somehow, it worked. Noonan scrambled down the truncated rope as far as he could go, and hung there, waiting. Dawes went next, descending the rope until his feet touched Noonan's shoulders, then carefully clambering down Noonan's body until he grasped the big man's feet.

'Okay, come on!' Noonan shouted. 'We can't hang this way forever!'

Dawes strained to hold on. His toes were about eight feet above the ground. Carol came down the rope; he could feel every impact as she descended. Looking up, he saw her coming down past Noonan's shoulders, then reaching his own shoulders. Her face was white with tension. She clung for an instant to Dawes' hips, slid down his legs, and let go. He glanced down; she had landed in a crumpled heap, but she was getting up.

Cherry came next. Dawes' arms ached mercilessly. He tightened his grip on Noonan's ankles. But it was no use; he could not hold on. As Cherry's foot grazed his shoulder, he let go and dropped to the ground. He folded up as he hit, but was able to rise without difficulty. Cherry still dangled from Noonan.

'Go ahead,' Dawes called to her. 'Let go and I'll catch you.'

She released her hold. Dawes braced himself and broke her fall, but the weight of her dropping on him knocked him over again. A moment later, Noonan landed on top of them.

After some instants of confusion, they struggled to their feet and began to laugh. Cherry was the first to start, and then Noonan and Dawes and Carol took it up, and they laughed for nearly a minute at the ridiculous spectacle they must have made, solemnly clambering down each other and landing in a heap.

'Damnedest silly way to get down a mountainside I ever saw,' Noonan said, still laughing.

'Maybe so,' Dawes said. 'But it worked, didn't it? It worked!'

They huddled together at the base of the cliff. Above them, two lengths of rope dangled in the wind.

Cherry said, 'And there isn't an alien in sight. Not anywhere.'

Dawes looked rapidly around, as if expecting to see the thick-bodied ape-like beings clustered behind trees observing them. Perhaps they were. But certainly they were keeping well out of sight.

'You see?' Dawes said triumphantly. 'They aren't interested in us any more. We don't have anything to offer them, now that we've stopped fighting with each other. They don't care what we do now.'

'I'm cold,' Carol said suddenly.

'We all are,' said Cherry. 'We better get a move on. Back to the colony, before the aliens decide they don't want to let us go after all.'

Dawes nodded. He pointed toward the forest. 'Standing with our backs to the cliff, the colony ought to be straight out that way. What do you think, Noonan?'

The big man frowned and said, 'That's about right. We ought to find our way back there through the forest without much trouble. If we start out now.'

'Right. We want to get there before nightfall,' Dawes

said. 'We've still got a few hours left. We'd better start out now.'

They set out, in single file – Noonan leading, followed by Carol, then Cherry and Dawes. Even though the sun was bright in the sky, the day was cold; the temperature was barely above fifty, Dawes estimated.

He was thankful that they had kept their shoes, even if their stockings all had gone to reinforce the rope. The forest floor was covered with the dried prickly cast-off needles of the conifer trees that abounded there. The wind whipped through the forest, but the trees served as shielding for them against the coldest blasts.

It had taken about two hours to go through the forest the first time, in the hands of the aliens. By Dawes' reckoning, nightfall was not due for at least three hours more. With luck, if they followed a true path, they would make it back to the colony before dark. Once night fell, of course, they would simply have to squat down and wait for morning before proceeding.

But Noonan led the way with such a confident air that Dawes did not worry. The big man strode along with springing step, looking back every few moments to make sure no one had fallen behind.

Dawes realized that a few months ago this whole sequence of events would have been inconceivable.

After an hour of walking, they stopped; Carol was exhausted. Noonan eyed the angle of the sun, wrinkled up his face, and announced that they had at least two and a half hours before sunset. 'Plenty of time to make it,' the big man added. 'If we don't waste any time en route.'

'I'm cold,' Carol said. 'Hungry. Tired. I can't keep walking like this.'

Dawes looked at her pityingly. She looked drawn and exhausted. Carol had taken the days in the cave worse than any of them. Noonan hardly showed a trace of his captivity; Cherry looked unkempt but healthy, with a sleek leanness that she had not had before. Dawes ached all over, but he felt splendid.

'Come on,' he said gently to Carol. 'We're almost there. Another hour's walk, that's all.'

Noonan lifted her to her feet and pointed her in the right direction. They resumed their hike.

They were following a path, well-worn through the thick forest. Looking back, Dawes could see the black bulk of the cliffs – and, he thought, the two strands of rope, red and yellow and brown and green. As the sun dropped, the forest became colder. Birds hooted in the trees; small shiny-skinned animals that looked like lizards sprang up on rocks, chittered derisively at the group for an instant, and went hustling off into the safety of the woods.

They plodded on. Dawes was beginning to feel the effects of his hunger – only one meal a day for the last five, and that not very nourishing. He longed to stop and try to shy a rock at one of the curious little forest beasts, but he told himself that if they ever stopped they might not get started again. He forced himself to drag one foot in front of the other. His legs ached. His feet, bare inside his shoes, were slowly being rubbed raw by the leather scraping his heel. But Noonan strutted jauntily along in the lead.

They were on their way back to the colony. Something strange and mysterious had happened to them, but it was over, and they were on their way back. Dawes comforted himself with that thought. In a little while, they would be seeing other people again. Haas and Dave Matthews and Ed Sanderson and Sid Nolan and all the others. They were really strangers to him, but at the moment Dawes thought of them as old friends, friends for whose companionship he had longed for months and years.

They stopped again a short time later. Again, it was Carol. She threw herself down on the ground, sobbing, muttering little senseless sounds.

Noonan scooped her up. Dawes hung back, even though technically she was his wife. She would have to be carried, and he had barely enough strength to carry himself along. Therefore, Noonan would have to carry her. It was as simple as that. Dawes made no protest as Noonan picked her up and cradled her roughly in his arms.

'We're almost there,' Noonan told them. 'I'll carry her the rest of the way. You two all right?'

'I'll make it,' Cherry said. 'If I don't freeze first, that is.'

'You, Dawes?'

'I'm okay.'

'Let's go, then.'

Step after step after step; and every step, Dawes told himself sternly, brought him that much closer to the colony, to food and warmth and clothing. Unless, of course, Noonan had been leading them in the wrong direction all this time. That might be. No, Dawes argued; the cliffs were still at their backs, and so they had to be going in the right direction. His tired mind thought up cold fantasies: suppose the aliens had been following them all this time, maliciously feeding on their suffering, and planned to massacre them as they stood within sight of the stockade? Or perhaps the stockade itself would be empty, all of the colonists dead or captured, leaving Dawes and Carol, Noonan and Cherry as the sole population of Osiris?

He shook away the thoughts and kept going. Abruptly they emerged into a clearing.

'Take a look,' Noonan said exultantly.

The stockade was a hundred yards ahead of them.

CHAPTER SEVENTEEN

Unsheathed gunsnouts greeted them as they appeared, footsore, dirty, chilled, at the colony stockades. The gunbarrels came snaking out of spyholes in the wall; the colonists were on guard now against any shapes of the forest, it seemed.

'Take it easy,' Noonan called out. 'We're friends. Humans.'

A voice said distinctly behind the stockade, 'Christ! Those aren't aliens! It's—'

'They've come back!' someone yelled.

The gunsnouts disappeared. The stockade gate creaked open and people came rushing out, familiar people, *friends*. Dawes recognized Sid Nolan, Dave Matthews, Matt Zachary, and Lee Donaldson. There were a few others whose names he could not at all remember.

They dragged the four returnees within, slammed the stockade gate shut. Marya Brannick appeared with blankets, and the wanderers were quickly clad. Inquisitive eyes goggled at the four weary ones. Questions bubbled up.

'Where were you?'

'What happened?'

'How did you get free?'

Dawes shook all the questioners off. 'Where's Haas?' he asked. 'We'd better talk to him first.'

Dave Matthews shook his head gravely. 'Haas – isn't here any more.'

'Did the aliens get him?' asked Noonan.

'No. Not the aliens.'

'Where *is* he, then?' Dawes demanded.

Matthews shrugged. 'We had some trouble here, after the aliens broke in and kidnapped you. Howard Stoker and a couple of his buddies thought Haas ought to quit as Colony Director. He – got killed.'

'Killed? So Stoker's in charge now?'

Matthews smiled gloomily. 'No. There was a – well, a counter-revolution, you might call it. In the name of law and order we executed Stoker, Harris and Hawes. Lee Donaldson's the Director now.'

'What's happening to the four surplus women, if those men are dead?'

'We're having trouble over that,' Matthews admitted. 'The colony's kind of split on the subject of polygamy right now. But—'

'Let our troubles wait till later,' Lee Donaldson broke in brusquely. ' I want to hear about these people. Where were you?'

'We were taken to a cave in one of the cliffs beyond the forest,' Dawes said. 'We were prisoners. The aliens were keeping us. But we escaped,' he grinned. He felt very tired after the forest trek, but yet invigorated. Tougher, harder. And he was saddened to learn that there had been dissension in the colony.

'Did they hurt you?' Donaldson asked.

Dawes thought about that for a moment. 'No,' he said finally. 'Not – not physically.'

He looked around. There hadn't been much progress in the colony in his absence. It still looked bare and hardly begun. He saw troubled faces. There had been bitter quarrelling here, he realized.

'What about the aliens?' he asked. 'Did they make any further attacks?'

163

'No,' Matthews said. 'We've seen them skulking around, outside the stockade. But they haven't tried to break in again. We keep a constant patrol, now.'

'And there's been trouble here, hasn't there?'

'Trouble?'

Dawes nodded. 'Arguments. Dissension.'

Lee Donaldson tightened his jaw muscles tensely. 'We've had some difficulties. Haas was our best leader, and he's dead. It hasn't been so easy to make the people work together since Stoker got his big idea. We do more arguing than working these days.'

Dawes sighed. He wanted to tell Matthews and Donaldson what they had learned in the cave, how the aliens thrived vicariously on strife, how the colonists would never be completely free of the shadowy neckless beings until they learned to function like parts of a well-machined instrument, as a colony must if it is to survive.

But there there was time for that later, he thought. You didn't make people see things in a minute, or in ten minutes. It could take days – or forever. But there was time to begin healing the colony's wounds later.

In a way, Dawes thought, it was a good thing that the colony had something like the aliens waiting outside to feed on their hate. It would be like having a perpetual visible conscience; hate would not enter the colony for fear of the aliens without.

He turned away. Suddenly he wanted to be alone with himself – with the *new* self that had come out of the cave. Something had grown with him in those five days, and it hadn't been just the silky beard stubbling his cheeks. It was something else.

He understood now why selection was necessary, why the seed of Earth had to be carried from world to world. It was because the stars were *there*, and because it was in the nature of man to climb outward, transcending himself, changing himself. As he had changed, for he *had* changed, in those few catalytic days in the cave.

They had been days of hardening for him. No longer was he filled with vague angry resentment; no longer did he hate selection and all its minions, Local Chairman Brewer and District Chairman Mulholland. He forgave them. More; he admired them, and pitied them because they had to stay behind in this greatest of all human adventures.

In the twilight Dawes walked away from the group, down toward the bubble-home he had chosen and from which he had been taken by the aliens. His suitcase and Carol's still lay half-open on the ground – the bubble hadn't been entered since the night of the kidnapping.

Shrugging out of the blanket, he took spare clothing from his suitcase and dressed slowly. He stood for a long time, thinking. They would none of them be the same any more – not Noonan, who for the first time in his life had run into a problem he couldn't solve with his fists, or Carol, who had gone into the cave innocent and come out otherwise, or Cherry, whose metal shell had broken open to give him a moment of tenderness.

But Dawes knew that he had changed most of all, and yet not changed. The thing that was inside him, the curiosity, the seeking mind – now, it was alive and truly working for the first time. How wrong it had been to dream of that cozy, dead existence in his nice Ohio home with his nice Ohio wife and his nice Ohio children! He realized now that he wanted to get out into the wilderness and see the aliens again, find out why they were the way they were, what they had wanted from the prisoners in the cave, how they had taken it, what they were really like. Osiris held a million mysteries. And through the miracle of selection he had been put here to solve them.

I'm different now.

It was a hard fact to assimilate. He realized with a jolt, looking at Carol's suitcase, that she was still his wife. He didn't want her any more. The boy Mike Dawes had been taken by her innocence and shyness, but that boy no longer existed. And he needed someone more solid, someone who could share problems with him instead of simply clinging dependently.

Someone was knocking outside the bubble.

'Come on in,' Dawes said.

It was Cherry.

She looked flustered and confused. 'You just walked away from everybody like that,' she said. 'You feeling okay, Mike?'

'I just wanted to think. I had to be by myself for a little while. I'm okay.'

She was looking at him earnestly. Glancing away, she saw the two suitcases.

'Carol's with Noonan,' she said.

'I figured as much,' said Dawes without a trace of a quiver in his voice. 'I don't care. Really, I don't.'

It was funny, he thought, how lousy deals turned out to be the biggest things in your life. Being picked by the lottery, and then being grabbed by the aliens on top of that. And losing your wife to a man like Noonan. And none of it mattered – each loss was a find, each finish a beginning.

An animal honked in the forest, and Dawes grinned. A whole world lay out there beyond the stockade, waiting to have its secrets pried open in the years to come. And he'd do it.

He said, 'If Noonan's with Carol – where are you going to stay, Cherry?'

'I haven't figured that out yet.'

He smiled. Carol had left her suitcase here, but nothing else. If Noonan could be happy with her, let him be.

Cherry stepped forward awkwardly. Dawes wanted to tell her that he forgave her and loved her and needed her, and that he saw through her toughness and through the scars life had left on her. But he couldn't say any of those things out loud, and he realized he wasn't finished growing up, quite yet. She would help him, though. And he would help her.

Funny. Getting picked in the lottery had seemed like the end of the world to him, once. But he couldn't have been more wrong.

He smiled at Cherry. The girl before him was like a stranger, even after the days in the cave. Everything was oddly brand new. He tipped her face up the inch or two that separated them in height, and kissed her, listening to the wind of the alien world – *his* world.

'Hello,' she said tenderly.

'Hello,' he said.

Also in Hamlyn Paperbacks

Poul Anderson

THE MAKESHIFT ROCKET

Knud Axel Syrup, chief engineer of the spaceship *Mercury Girl*, sat and drank his favourite beer and thought about the coming war he was so anxious to avoid. For Grendel – the planetoid on which he was stranded – had been occupied by a band of fiery Irish revolutionaries. And once the rival Anglians discovered this, their response would be speedy and violent.

Then, as Herr Syrup shook up a bottle of brew and let the foam shoot out of its top, he realized suddenly what could be done to get him off Grendel.

And so came about a marvellous spaceship – built of beer kegs, bound by gunk, upholstered with pretzel boxes, and powered by the mighty reaction forces of malted brew!